A JAM
SCHOO

ELISABETH BATT

LUTTERWORTH PRESS · LONDON

First paperback edition 1972

ISBN 0 7188 1944 6

Printed in Great Britain
by Fletcher & Son Ltd, Norwich

CONTENTS

Chapter 1

MORNING IN JAMAICA

THERE were two tiny rooms in Pauline's house; the sleeping-room with the big bed in which Mama slept with Julie and baby Owen, and the living-room where Pauline's little bed was pushed against the wall. The first rays of the morning sun shone through the small square window of the living-room, so that Pauline was usually the first member of the family to awaken. But one morning she woke to find Mama holding her by the shoulders and gently shaking her.

"Wake up," she was saying. "Come now, Pauline, wake up. My—how the child sleep'!"

"O-oh—Mama! What time is it? Have I overslept?" Pauline rubbed her eyes and peered up at the cheap tin clock, noisily ticking on the shelf "But—'tisn't six, yet! Why are we to get up early to-day?" she protested.

Seeing that she was really awake at last, Mama hurried into the other room, where the baby was wailing loudly.

"Hurry, now, and dress. I'll tell you why when you've finished your duties," she called back through the open door. "There's something I want you to do for me on your way to school; something you'll like. But there'll not be time if you don't hurry yourself!"

School started at nine; the children were expected to arrive a quarter of an hour earlier, and it took Pauline half an hour to walk there. But, like most of her friends, she had to perform certain duties before leaving home.

She had more to do than some of the other girls because, since Father had died, Mama had nobody to help her. Julie was only four, but Pauline was nearly eleven and strong for her age. So besides making her bed and setting the table for breakfast, she was expected to fetch the water, milk Nanny the goat, and feed the hens—bringing in the eggs if there were any. Milking the goat took longer than all the other jobs put together, and Pauline always tackled this immediately she had drawn the water. But first she put on her oldest dress, which would be changed for a clean one before she set out for school. The old dress was too small for her and had been torn in several places, but the bright yellow colour looked fine against her shining black skin—for Pauline was a Jamaican girl.

Jamaica is an island where there is no winter; and, although it was February now, it was as hot as an English midsummer day. As Pauline stepped out through the door, she could not resist pausing for a moment to sniff the early morning freshness, and to watch the humming-birds already hovering over the scarlet flowers on the poinsettia bush.

"Make haste now!" called Mama, and Pauline picked up the bucket and pattered barefoot along the track which led to the rainwater tank, or catchment, behind the house. After carrying the water to Mama, she took some vegetable-peelings to the goat, who was tethered to a post higher up the hillside on which the house stood.

While Nanny was greedily eating the peelings, Pauline sat on a wooden box and milked her into a chipped jug. She was anxious to finish before the goat became restless, so she never once raised her head to look at the sunlit plain below, nor at the distant mountains. When the jug was full of fresh frothy milk, she carried it carefully down the steep slope, but stopped beside her mother, who was busy at the cooking-stove outside the house.

"Please Mama—tell me!" she pleaded. "What is the nice thing I'm to do to-day?"

"Get on and take that milk inside," Mama said smiling. "And use your eyes—instead of asking questions."

Pauline hurried into the living-room, and there on the table was a string of ripe oranges, tied up ready for market. Mama had picked them from the tree which grew near the house, and strung them by their stalks to a strip of split palm-leaf; and now Pauline knew why she had to get up early this morning. Mama was often short of

money, and she sometimes sent Pauline off with
something to sell at the market in the town on her
way to school; cobs of corn, or some sweet potatoes from the "patch" in front; oranges, bananas
or "ackees" from the grove of trees at the back of
the house. It was always fun to visit the market,
and Pauline needed no further urging to hurry
over her work. The earlier she started, the more
time there would be to watch the country folk setting up their stalls.

The hens had been busy, so there were fried
eggs with the fried johnny-cakes for breakfast.
Mama sat in a chair with Owen on her knee; Julie
had the other chair, and Pauline perched on the
bed. As soon as she had finished, she changed into
her red and white striped cotton dress, washed in
the bowl of cold water in the bedroom, then tried
to stand patiently while Mama brushed and
combed her frizzy black hair before parting it in
several places and braiding it into six wiry little
plaits, tied with red bows.

"Prayers, now," said Mama; and kneeling at the
table, where Pauline and Julie knelt on either side
of her, she asked for God's blessing on the day, and
all three said the Lord's Prayer. Then she read
aloud from the Bible, after which it was time for
Pauline to start. She picked up the bag woven of
split palm-leaves, which contained her slate, school-
books and sewing, and Mama handed her the
string of oranges.

"There's a dozen there," she said. "Mind and don't let them go for less than ninepence . . . and get a shilling for them if you can."

Pauline ran down the steep track which led to the road below, sometimes giving a little skip for sheer happiness. There were several small houses like her own dotted about the hillside, and where the track met the road she passed Mrs. Grant's big house where Mama would be going to work later in the morning, taking the two younger children with her.

The road was dusty, and already the heat of the sun was beginning to penetrate the early morning coolness, but Pauline kept on running. Mama had given her threepence for her lunch, which usually consisted of a bun and an "icicle" from the bakery near the school; but she thought now that it would be more fun to buy something to eat off one of the market stalls. Then, instead of going to the bakery during recess, she would spend some extra time working on the cloth she was embroidering for the school competition.

For a while she had the road to herself; then she overtook old Mrs. Harris, sitting sideways on her donkey which had two large panniers hanging one on each side of its back. One pannier was filled with sweet potatoes, the other held ackees—a bright red fruit which grows on trees and tastes very good when cooked and eaten as a vegetable. Mrs. Harris wore a white blouse and a long full skirt which was the same colour as the ackees. A large white handkerchief was tied round her head.

"'Morning, Mistress," said Pauline politely, as she came alongside the little donkey. "You taking your ackees to market?"

"Yes—and the taters, too," nodded the old woman, while her large black face crinkled into a broad smile. "You've some nice oranges there, I see. You shouldn't take them in too early!" she added, winking at the girl. "I hear there are visitors from England staying in the town . . . and you'd get a fancy price from them folks. But they won't be there this early. I'd wait a bit, if I was you."

"Can't wait, Mistress Harris. Got to be in school by nine, you know," laughed Pauline, running on ahead of the plodding donkey. A mule-cart passed her, laden with bright-green bananas which would later be ripened in the sun by those who bought them. Turning a bend in the road she saw Anna Scott striding along in the distance, with a big basket of oranges balanced on her head. Oranges! So many people here had oranges to sell. Pauline would be lucky if she got ninepence for her lot . . . unless—unless she played truant from school, and waited till later in the morning when the English visitors from the big hotel sometimes came to visit the market? Mistress Harris was right; these tourists never seemed to mind how high a price they paid. And if she missed school

for once, Teacher would think she had been
needed at home. It was too early, yet, for there to
be other schoolchildren on the road. There was
no one to give her away; no one to tell Teacher
that they had seen Pauline Cole going to the market. But then—there was her competition needlework! She couldn't get on without the new scarlet
silk Teacher had promised to get for her. This
was to brighten up the tablecloth she was embroidering, which, though prettily designed and
beautifully worked, was rather colourless—by
Jamaican standards. Still—there were two weeks
yet before the competition; one day lost wouldn't
make all that difference. And she *did* want to go
to the market . . . to spend the whole of the
morning there, instead of having to hurry away
just when the fun was beginning.

She walked more and more slowly, scuffing her
bare feet in the red dust at the roadside. She had
almost—very nearly quite—made up her mind to
miss school . . . when she saw something that
made her stand quite still with an angry exclama-
tion. To the right of the road a footpath crossed
a stretch of common land, and along this path a
boy was running. It was Mark Bailey, who was the
same age as Pauline and in her class at school. If
he had been a friend of hers she might have begged
him not to tell on her, and even tried to persuade
him to play truant as well. But he was a serious
boy, quiet and very shy, and never mixed much

with the other children. It was impossible to know what he was thinking, or whether or not he could be trusted to keep a secret.

Bother Mark Bailey! Why did he have to set out for school so early . . . and why was he coming from that direction—from Rocky Valley, instead of from his home which was up the hill on the opposite side of this road? Even as she wondered, she saw Mark stop in his tracks as if he had just caught sight of her; then he stepped quickly off the path and dodged behind a clump of low-growing bushes. The common was dotted with trees and shrubs, coconut-palms and thatch-palms, breadfruit trees and flame-of-the-forest trees with their huge orange-coloured flowers; pimento trees and bushes of scarlet or rose-coloured hibiscus. It was easy enough to hide and remain hidden. At one moment there had been a boy running along the footpath towards the main road; at the next moment the common appeared to be deserted. Pauline gave a low chuckle of delight. If Mark had something he wanted kept secret, he wouldn't be likely to tell on anyone else. Her mind was made up as she skipped along the road towards the town. She would not sell her oranges to the first people who asked for them; she would roam about the stalls, enjoying herself; and later in the morning she would get a high price for the fruit, perhaps even more than Mama had expected.

As she drew near to the town, she overtook

several women walking along with baskets balanced
on their heads, and she in her turn was overtaken
by mulecarts and pannier-laden donkeys. Everyone was gay and merry, calling out to each other,
and laughing so that their even, white teeth
gleamed in their dark faces. There was nothing
unusual in this; whether it was market day or not,
it was rare to see anyone in Jamaica without a ready
smile. The sun shone, and the flowers by the way-
side or in the gardens at the outskirts of the town
matched the gaudy dresses of the women and the
shirts worn by the men. In the town itself, the
streets were already crowded so that sometimes it
was difficult to get along. A car passed, sending
up clouds of dust and hooting at the donkeys and
foot people who were in no hurry to get out of the
way. Pauline laughed with delight. This was
better than sitting in school, doing sums which
seldom came out right, and learning about people
who had lived hundreds of years ago.

She pushed her way through the crowds and
mounted the stone steps to the Market Hall. This
was open at the sides, but had a roof overhead to
protect the stalls from the burning sun. The aisles
between the rows of stalls were thronged with
people, though the serious buying and selling had
not yet begun. The stall-holders were setting out
their wares . . . hats and baskets made of split
palm-leaf; huge circles of tobacco; gaily-coloured
dresses, shirts and handkerchiefs hung on strings;

great earthenware bowls filled with eggs, grain, peas and beans, rice or sweet potatoes; mountains of fruit—lemons, grapefruit, limes, and several kinds of oranges. There were fruits that we never see in England—pawpaws, which are rather like melons; and star-apples, the size and shape of our own apples, but tasting like ripe figs. Pauline spent one penny of her lunch money at the ice-cream stall; sucking her "icicle"—which is like an iced lolly—she wriggled her way through the jostling crowd, often pausing to gaze at the stalls on either side of her. One old woman was selling strings of beads, bracelets and ear-rings made of shells and seeds; she had no stall, but walked about carrying a tray laden with her wares, the strings of beads slung round her neck. Another woman edged her way through the throng carrying a live cockerel under her arm. The noise was deafening; everybody seemed to be shouting at once. But most of them were cheerful and good-humoured, and Pauline grinned happily at everyone who caught her eye.

Up and down the alleyways she wandered, and at last came out into the blazing sunshine at the back of the Market Hall. Here was a kind of yard in which people unloaded their donkeys or mule-carts. The patient donkeys were tethered in a row beyond, beneath the shade of a group of trees, but in the open space of the yard all was confusion, and the ground was thick with refuse. At the foot of the steps leading up to the hall were enormous heaps of green bananas; these had been brought wrapped in their own broad leaves, which now littered the yard. With her bare feet hidden by the dry rustling banana-leaves, Pauline stood and watched the brilliant scene, always changing but always gay and colourful. Blue, pink and purple, yellow, orange and scarlet . . . Jamaicans love to wear the vivid colours that suit them so well.

Some ragged children from the hills were crowding round a small donkey which had just entered the yard. A little boy was perched on its back between the panniers filled with bananas and sweet corn—emerald-green bananas and orange-coloured corn—and it was led by a tall woman with a bright handkerchief tied turban-wise round her crinkled black hair. Pauline ran across to join the other children, and saw a fair-skinned lady talking to the woman with the donkey. She held a camera, and was asking, very politely, if she might take a photograph of the donkey with its panniers and with the little boy on top.

"You'll have to pay me, Mistress," retorted the woman. "A shilling—give me a shilling, and you shall take a picture." A boy leading another donkey pushed his way roughly through the group. "You better take a picture of my donkey, Missis," he shouted. "My donkey is bigger—and you can do it for sixpence!"

Pauline was not in the least embarrassed by this

B

scene. The market was always full of rough people who came in from the surrounding countryside, and these thought nothing of begging or of getting what they could out of the English or American tourists. This English lady ignored the boy and continued to talk to the woman as if there had been no interruption.

"I will give you a shilling," she said. "Not for taking the photograph, but because I hope you will spend it on a new halter for your donkey. This cord is cutting his mouth . . . see, it's bleeding."

She gently touched the poor beast's velvety nose, then began loosening the knot of the rope which had been clumsily tied into a substitute for a halter. Pauline pressed closer, for this was something quite unusual. She herself had often felt unhappy at seeing the careless way animals were treated— live chickens brought to market and left gasping in the sun, overloaded donkeys, a lame mule draw- ing a heavy load of sugar-cane—but she had never met anyone else who felt as she did. This woman, however, spoke of the donkey as if it were a human being. The donkey's owner looked sullen and muttered something under her breath; but the lady smiled at her and said: "A faithful servant deserves kind treatment." Then, having eased the cord, she took a tin of ointment from her bag, and applied a little of it to the animal's sore mouth. At this, the woman's eyes nearly started out of her head, and the onlookers gasped. Ointment from the chemist's shop—which must have cost a lot of money! And all for a mere donkey!

"I'm sure you wouldn't want to cause pain to one of God's creatures," the lady said gently, and was moving away when Pauline stepped in front of her.

"Ripe oranges, Mistress; beautiful oranges!" she chanted, holding up the string of fruit. This lady must be rich—and not only rich, but generous. It was too good a chance to be missed.

"Good sound oranges, every one! Fresh gathered this morning. You'll see none like them in the whole market," she urged.

"I've seen hundreds, exactly like them," smiled the lady. "Even growing on the trees in the garden where I'm staying! But still—these look very tempting. How much do you want for them?"

"Two shillings," Pauline said boldly. "Two shillings for the twelve . . . I couldn't take less, sweet and juicy as they are."

"Two shillings," the stranger repeated thoughtfully. "That's twopence each; they'd cost twice that amount in England, and these really are beauties. Here—I'll take the whole string."

For a moment, Pauline was completely taken aback. Expecting the customer to haggle with her, she had mentioned a ridiculously high price. She would have been delighted if she had succeeeded in getting sixpence or even threepence above the shilling Mama had hoped for. Grinning broadly, she handed over the oranges, and her small black fingers closed over the two separate shillings.

" Do you live near here? " asked the lady. " Will you be coming to any of the Mission services? "

Pauline stared at her without speaking. She vaguely remembered hearing something in Sunday School about a Mission; but she had not been attending, and now her mind was busy trying to decide how to spend her extra shilling. She was soon separated from her customer by a crowd of Jamaicans who hoped to get as good a price for their wares as Pauline had done. She tied Mama's shilling into a corner of her handkerchief and dropped it into her basket, keeping the other coin grasped tightly in her hand. At the back of her mind was the unwelcome thought that this extra shilling rightly belonged to her mother, who needed it badly. But she succeeded in stifling this uncomfortable feeling, and hurried back into the Market Hall. She still had twopence left of her lunch money; should she spend that on sweets for Julie, and the shilling on a pretty cotton head-square for herself? But it wouldn't do to take anything home; Mama would see it, and ask how she came by the money to buy it. Besides, she was beginning to feel very hungry and thirsty. It would be better to spend some of the money on a really good feast, and save the rest for another time.

She spent one penny on some sugar-coated bis-

cuits, and another on a big slice of melon. Taking
bites from these, turn and turn about, she
dawdled up and down the stalls for hours, unable
to make up her mind. She was tempted by the
beads, and longed for one of the shell bracelets;
but these would be difficult to hide when she went
home. The sight of a bundle of sugar-cane set her
mouth watering; but there were cane-fields near
her home, and she was often given a piece to chew.
It would be silly to waste money on what she could
get for nothing. It was a great responsibility having a whole shilling to spend; without quite realizing it, Pauline was not feeling as happy and light-
hearted as she had felt before. However, she had
all day in which to make her choice.

She decided to eat the rest of her biscuits away
from the crowd, in the shady place where the donkeys were tethered. It was nice to get away from
the glare and the noise, and she always loved to be
with animals. She gave half a sugar-biscuit to the
thinnest donkey and fondled his furry ears, remembering what the lady had said about them being
"God's creatures". How beautiful it would be,
she thought, to go about secretly helping all the
unhappy, ill-treated animals; giving water to
neglected fowls, comforting dogs which were kept
chained up all day. But there were so few that she
could help; her heart ached to think of all the
hundreds of dumb beasts whose sufferings she
could not relieve. If only they could be made

happy and gay, like the human beings who were chattering and jostling each other in the yard.

But, even as she looked at the ever-moving crowd, she saw a blind man tapping his white stick on the ground as he made his way towards the corner where he would sit during the rest of the day, waiting for what anyone cared to give him. A very old woman, so thin that she seemed to be nothing but skin and bone, crouched on the edge of the steps. Someone tossed her a coin—so carelessly that it rolled to the foot of the steps, where an urchin pounced on it, and ran off laughing triumphantly. A small child, forgotten by his thoughtless mother, was crying bitterly because he was lost. He was so tiny, not much bigger than Pauline's brother Owen, and already he had been knocked down and trodden on by careless hurrying feet. Pauline ran to pick him up, but when she reached the place where he had been, he had disappeared. She hoped that his mother had found him, but could not be sure.

All the brightness seemed to have gone out of the day, for all that the sun shone so fiercely; there was so much suffering in the world—not only among animals but human beings, too. She had never felt quite like this before. It was the lady who had first made her begin to notice these things . . . the lady whom Pauline had cheated of the shilling which she ought, now, to hand over to her mother. Somehow, Pauline knew that she couldn't

start helping sad people and being kind to neglected animals while she was all wrong inside. The
two things just didn't go together.

"I don't care," she muttered to herself. "I'm
going to spend the shilling . . . I can't give it up
now. But to-morrow I'll start being good."

Without thinking of where she was going, she
had wandered to the edge of the market square,
and now found herself opposite the little gate
which led into the back of the churchyard. Near
this gate several people were crowding round a
grown-up girl who seemed to be selling something.

"A shilling," Pauline heard her say. "They're
only a shilling each.

She held a pile of small brown books, and suddenly Pauline knew that a book was exactly what
she wanted to buy. She would always have it, it
would last for ever; and her mother would think
someone at school had lent it to her, so there would
be no awkward questions asked. She held out her
shilling, and received a book in exchange, then
quickly looked away on realizing that the big girl
was Judith Holmes, one of the assistant Sunday
School teachers. Pauline slipped the book into
her bag, and ran back into the crowd. It was just
possible that Judith didn't know her by name, as
she taught the youngest class, but it was no use
running risks. In fact, it wouldn't be safe to stay
much longer at the market. Soon the children
would be coming out of school, and some of them

would be sure to visit the market before going home. One of them might tell Teacher that Pauline Cole had not been kept at home to help her mother . . . that she had been seen amusing herself at the market.

In any case, there was no point in lingering among the stalls now that she had no money left. Besides, she wanted to see what her new book was about, and she couldn't look at it properly with all these people pushing and elbowing her. She would find a peaceful spot outside the town, and have a nice read until it was time to go home.

She made her way out into the country, walking fast as if, by hurrying, she could escape from her own thoughts. She didn't want to admit, even to herself, that her stolen holiday had been a little disappointing. But she felt a pang of envy for her carefree schoolfellows who had spent the hottest part of the day in a cool, airy schoolroom, and would now be enjoying themselves at the market or hurrying home to tea, with nothing weighing on their minds. Alice and Jennifer, her chief rivals in the needlework competition, would have been able to get forward with their work, while hers was still in her basket. She couldn't even make up for lost time now, because she hadn't got the fresh supply of embroidery silk. And the market had not, after all, been so very much fun, after the first hour or so. It had been so hot and crowded . . .

and there had been the poor old woman and the blind man and the little lost child. In these and other ways Pauline tried to account for the mood of depression which had settled on her, rather than face the real reason for her sadness.

Chapter 2

MARK'S ESCAPE

SHE turned off the road and climbed the hill till she reached the shade of a group of bread-fruit trees. Here she sat down and opened the little brown book . . . only to find that it was not a story-book, after all. It was a hymn-book. A loose printed sheet of paper inside the cover informed her that these were the hymns to be used throughout the Mission; and there was a list of places at which the Mission services were to be held—at 7.30 every evening. In any other circumstances, she would have been thrilled to possess a hymn-book of her very own. To her, as to most of her friends, Sunday School followed by the Service in the Parish Church were the most important events of the week. Not for anything would she have missed Church on Sunday, even though she did not always understand it or attend very closely. She always listened to the reading from the Bible, however, because this was the link between Church and home. She had never known a day when a portion of the Bible had not been read in her home, and it was the same in the houses of her friends.

It was somehow comforting and reassuring to hear the same words being read in the great Church, as part of a solemn service. Though the service was not always solemn. Some of the hymns were gay and joyous; and with every member of the congregation joining in the singing, it made you feel ready to burst with happiness.

It was wonderful to own a hymn-book. And on the very page at which she opened it, was a hymn she knew well.

"There is a green hill far away," she sang softly, her eyes on the distant hills across the valley, for she knew the words by heart.

> "Where the dear Lord was crucified,
> Who died to save us all.
> We may not know, we cannot tell
> What pains He had to bear.
> But we believe it was for us . . ."

Her voice faltered, and she paused, then went on to the next verse.

> "He died that we might be forgiven;
> He died to make us good;
> That we might go at last to Heaven
> Saved by His precious blood.
> There was no other good enough . . ."

It was no use; she just didn't feel like singing that hymn to-day. Overleaf there was one of her favourites: "Loving Shepherd." But as she sang:

" Teach Thy Lamb Thy voice to hear; suffer not my steps to stray,"—her eyes filled with tears.

> " Loving Saviour, Thou didst give
>   Thine own life that we might live . . ."

. . . She turned over some more pages quickly. Surely the hymns in this book were not all sad ones?   No—here was a splendid one.

> " There were ninety and nine that safely lay
>   In the shelter of the fold.
>   But one had wandered far away . . ."

She shut the book angrily.   The words seemed to be hurting her on purpose—trying to make her unhappy.   She had a good mind to throw the book into the bushes, and run home and forget about it.   But it was such a neat little book—and the pages had a lovely new smell . . . and it had cost a whole shilling.   She opened it again, and started to read a hymn that was new to her.

> " It is a thing most wonderful,
>   Almost too wonderful to be,
>   That God's own Son came down from Heaven
>   And died, to save a child like me.
>   I cannot see how He could love
>   A child so weak and full of sin.
>   His love must be most wonderful
>   If He could die, my love to win.
>   . . . I sometimes think about the Cross . . ."

"*No!*" She was nearly sobbing now. "I don't want to! I *won't* think about it!" Why was there so much dreadfulness in the world? At first glance, it was all so beautiful; but when you looked again, there were ill-treated animals and lost, frightened children, blind men, starving old women—and—a girl who sold her mother's oranges and kept back some of the money for herself.

Pauline stood up and looked wildly round, trying to escape from the thoughts which were pressing in on her. Some boys were running along the road below her, and she watched them, glad to have something new to think about. They stopped at the place where she herself had paused that morning, when she had seen Mark Bailey running along the path across the common on the other side of the road. They stared up the hill and all around, as if they were on the look-out for some-one. Then, like Mark, they too crept into a clump of bushes and hid there. Pauline wondered rather nervously whether they were waiting for her. They were bigger than she was and there were four of them; if they meant to torment her, she would be helpless. She glanced around to find a way home by which she could avoid meeting them; and at that moment, Mark Bailey appeared over the brow of the hill above her, and came running down the slope. He carried a basket which she guessed must contain food, as it was covered by a white

cloth. She realized, then, that the boys were waiting for Mark, perhaps meaning to rob him of whatever he was carrying.

" Hist—Mark! Mark Bailey," she called softly,
running to meet him. " Stop—don't go down to
the road. There are four big boys, hiding in the
bushes there." He had stopped dead at the first
sound of her voice; now he came towards her
slowly, looking nervous and embarrassed.

" Where are they? " he muttered.

" Down in that clump there." She pointed to
the place where she had last seen them. " Where
are you going? " she asked. " Can't you get round
by some other way? "

He hesitated; then: " I'm going to my Granny's,"
he said. " She lives in Rocky Valley. Yes—I can
go the longer way round. Thanks, Pauline."
He was making off, but she put a hand on his arm.

" Were you coming from your Granny's this
morning? " she asked. " I saw you crossing the
common, when I was on the road. And—and you
stopped when you saw me, and hid in the bushes."

At first she thought he was going to flare up in
anger; then, avoiding her eyes, he said: " I always
try and keep out of sight when I'm going there or
coming back. Sometimes they try and get the
basket from me . . . I don't often go the same
way twice running, since they got to know about
me going down there."

" Do you go there every day? Is your Granny

ill?" she wanted to know. She did not mean to be inquisitive, but she was always interested in other people.

Mark looked as if he were not sure whether or not she was to be trusted. He began to say something, stopped; started again . . . but suddenly both children were startled by a shout from the road below. The four boys had come out from their hiding-place, and now one of them was pointing at Mark and Pauline.

Calling: "You get on home as fast as you can, Pauline," Mark turned and sprinted down the hill at an angle, aiming for a point further along the road. The others set off in hot pursuit; but he had taken them by surprise and had such a good start that they were unable to cut him off before he reached the road. They followed him, however; he was smaller than they were and handicapped by his basket, and it seemed unlikely that he would be able to keep up that pace for much longer. Pauline watched till they were out of sight. They were like a pack of fierce cruel animals, she thought with a shiver.

The air was cooler now, and the plain below was bathed in that soft, golden glow which comes a little while before sunset. But the beauty of the evening seemed, to Pauline, a little sad compared with the fresh loveliness of morning—when the day was new, and there had not yet been time for all the cruelty and fear and unhappiness to spoil it.

Chapter 3

THE WAY OF DECEIT

AS soon as she was within sight of home, Julie came running to meet her.

"Here she is, Mama! Here she is!" she called over her shoulder. "Where've you been, Paulie? I've been watching out for you ever so long," she complained, pulling at her sister's hand.

"Whatever have you been doing, child? You know I've told you and told you to come straight home from school," Mama scolded. She was wearing her best dress and her bright pink Sunday hat. "I suppose you went back to the market again after school," she went on, not waiting for Pauline to answer. "How much did you get for the oranges? A shilling? That's a good girl . . . and now— get on with your little duties, then wash and tidy yourself, else I'll have to leave you behind."

"Why? What—where are we going, Mama?" Pauline asked listlessly, trying to stifle the uncomfortable feeling that had attacked her when she handed over the shilling.

"The Mission service is to be at Treetop Hill this evening. I haven't been able to get to any of the others, since I've no one to leave the children with. But this one's so near, we can take them with us."

Treetop Hill was the name of the nearest "village"—though there was no village, such as we know in England, to be seen; simply a little shop or store which served the houses—some no better than huts—in the surrounding district. Julie was already dressed in her snowy-white frock and straw poke-bonnet decorated with a wreath of flowers, and Mama was washing Owen's face while she talked.

"You've never been to an open-air Mission service," she continued. "I used to love them when I was a girl. Now—get on with the milking, and feed the hens and eat your supper. Maybe we'll meet someone there who'll be willing to take you on the other nights. The Mission's going on for another two weeks."

While Pauline milked the goat, she was thinking of the lady who had asked her if she had been to any of the Mission services. And there had been the notice in the hymn-book, too; but both these things reminded her of the extra shilling that she had kept for herself . . . which was just what she was trying to forget.

Going to an open-air service would be something new and exciting, and would perhaps drive away unwelcome thoughts. She hurried through her home duties, washed and tidied herself by the light

C

of the oil lamp, then quickly ate the dish of rice-and-peas which had been put ready for her; the others had already finished their supper.

She was about to eat the last mouthful when Mama picked up her school bag saying: "Let's see how your competition embroidery is coming on." She was secretly proud of Pauline's needlework and longed to see it win the competition. "Did the red silk brighten it up, like Teacher said it would?" Pauline choked over her mouthful and gulped down some water.

"I—I—Teacher couldn't get the red silk for to-day," she stammered. "She—she'll have it to-morrow, she says. I couldn't do any work today . . . I can't get on without the new silk, you see."

"Oh well——!" Disappointed, Mama put the work back into the bag; then she picked up baby Owen, took Julie by the hand, and told Pauline to bring the electric torch. There are no long light evenings in Jamaica even in their summertime; no lingering twilight. Now, at half-past six, it was already quite dark. Led by Pauline with the torch, they followed the track which ran up the hill till it joined the narrow roadway. They trudged along, always uphill, and were soon overtaken by a party of neighbours who were also going to Tree-top Hill. Pauline, now carrying Julie, listened to the grown-ups talking about the Mission.

"Pity you couldn't have been there on the other

THE WAY OF DECEIT

nights Mistress Cole," one of them said to her
mother. "The Missioner is a gentleman from
England; he and his wife are stopping with Archdeacon at the Rectory."

"The Missioner is a lovely preacher," said another. "A real man of God; the grandest preacher
I've ever heard."

"I remember the missions when I was a girl;
those were the days when you heard lovely preach-
ing," sighed Pauline's mother.

"You'll hear as good again to-night," promised
one of the neighbours. "We sing all the old
Gospel hymns, too. It's only the young folks that
need to follow the words when the singing starts;
we old ones don't need a book! "

Pauline pressed her hand against the front of
her dress down which she had hidden her own
private hymn-book. It felt awkward and uncomfortable—like the weight on her heart because of
the lie she had told Mama about the embroidery.
She was a truthful child on the whole; and it
puzzled her to remember how naturally and easily
the lie had slipped out—without her having to
think about it. As if she had been in the habit of
telling untruths every day. She began to see, now,
how one thing had led to another; first, playing
truant from school; then taking all that money
from an English lady who couldn't be expected to
know that she was being cheated. Keeping the
extra money for herself, instead of taking it to

Mama, had followed on quite naturally after that . . . and so had the deceitfulness about the needlework. It was like getting a sickness; you started with a sore throat, then a headache, then you had stomache-ache or came out in spots or sores—according to the kind of sickness you had caught. There seemed no way of ending it once you had caught the infection.

Chapter 4

THE MISSION

SEVERAL other people had joined them, so that there was quite a crowd by the time they arrived at Treetop Hill. But a far larger crowd had already assembled round the tilley-lamp which hung over the door of the store. The light shone on a table and two chairs directly below it, and it cast a wide circle of light in which the people stood waiting for the preacher. Small children ran in and out among them, but the bigger ones stood with their elders, quiet and expectant. The light picked out the brilliant colours of women's and children's dresses and men's shirts. Beyond the circle of light, the dark faces merged into the shadows and would have been invisible but for the bright eyes and gleaming white teeth. Fireflies flitted about in the blackness beyond, and here and there a stationary light showed where houses were scattered over the hillside. Suddenly someone held up a hand, saying:

"Listen! Can you hear them?"

The low murmur of talk died down—and now Pauline could hear, faint and very far away, the sound of music. It was a hymn: "Softly and tenderly Jesus is calling"—sung by a great choir; and it was getting louder—coming nearer and nearer with incredible swiftness. Julie seized Pauline's hand and looked up, her face radiant.

"It's the angels!" she whispered. "They're coming, Paulie—they're getting quite near! They'll be here, soon!"

She began to skip up and down with excitement, but Pauline pressed closer to her mother. Of course it wasn't angels, really; she didn't believe that for a moment. But—if they weren't angels— *who were they*? How could such a vast crowd of singers move so fast? She could even catch some of the words they were singing, now.

"—Jesus is calling, calling to you and to me . . ." And then the chorus: "Come home! Come home! . . . Calling—O sinner, come home!"

Softly, the crowd round the lamp took up the next verse—and soon everyone was singing. Singly, or by twos and threes, people were approaching quickly from all directions—from up the hill and from down the hill, singing as they walked. They were those who lived near by and had stayed at home till the service was due to begin; but it seemed as if they came in answer to the words of the chorus: "Come home! Come home!"

The music which had drawn them was very close now, very loud; in another moment it would be in their midst. Pauline's large eyes rolled from side to side, looking wildly for some way of escape. If these were really angels, it meant that the Lord Jesus was coming again . . . like it said in the Bible—"with all His angels". Pauline had been taught that the Coming of the Lord might happen at any moment . . . but somehow she had always assumed that it wouldn't be for a long long time. When He came, He would gather together all those who belonged to Him—who were His own; but the others—the ones who were disobedient and who cheated and told lies would be left out; left in something terrible called Outer Darkness. She had heard all this without thinking very much about it. And now it was actually happening. In a moment a great cry would be heard: "The Master cometh!" And she wasn't ready. She wasn't ready!

There was a blinding light . . . but it was only from the headlamps of a car which came up the road and turned into the space in front of the store. Three people sat in the front seat, Archdeacon and two others; and on the back seat was a gramophone playing the record of the hymn. A loudspeaker fixed to the roof of the car amplified the noise so that it could be heard from a long way off. But such a large crowd had gathered now that their singing rivalled the recorded music. And more and more were arriving. The record in the car had been changed; everyone was singing: "Hark,

Hark my soul." When they came to the verse
with the words:

"The voice of Jesus sounds o'er land and sea.
And laden souls by thousands meekly stealing,
Kind Shepherd, turn their weary steps to Thee . . ."

Pauline shed tears of relief. Relief—but also
shame and sorrow that she should have actually
not wanted the Lord to come. When she went
home after the service, she would tell Mama everything. No matter how bad the punishment, she
could not go through the night with this sin uncon-
fessed. And then she would kneel down and ask
for God's forgiveness. She would say: "Lord, be
merciful to me, a sinner."

Her tears had half-blinded her; but now she
saw the tall figure of Archdeacon standing by the
table under the lamp, holding up his hand for
silence. Beside him stood a fair man, who was
nearly as tall as Archdeacon. He had merry blue
eyes and a kind smile, and Pauline liked him on
sight. Near to him his wife sat on one of the
chairs. She had turned to greet one of the Church
workers who stood behind the chair, her arms full
of hymn-books. Those who could afford a shilling
had been buying these books; usually three or four
people had joined together and were sharing one
book between them. Just as Archdeacon gave out
the number of the first hymn—"Tell me the old,
old story,"—the Missioner's wife turned round,

and Pauline saw her face. It was a face she had seen before, that morning, in the market. This was the lady who had been taking photographs . . . who had been sorry for the poor donkey . . . and who had bought Pauline's oranges.

Pauline edged her way back through the crowd, leaving Julie standing beside Mama. She was terrified now lest the lady should see her and perhaps give some sign of recognition. Mama would notice at once; she would want to know when Pauline had met the English lady . . . and maybe the whole story would come out before there had been a chance to own up. It was safer to be at the back, concealed behind some of the big people, and she could hear perfectly well from there.

Archdeacon had said a prayer, and all had joined in the Our Father; and then he read from the Bible. It was the story of the Good Samaritan which most of them knew by heart; nearly every man, woman and child said the words aloud, quietly, while the Archdeacon read them. Then he closed the Bible and said that he would ask Mr. Elliot, the Missioner, to talk to them about what he had been reading.

At first Pauline had some difficulty in understanding what Mr. Elliot said, because his voice and way of speaking were so different from the Jamaican way. But she got used to it after a while; he was talking about the two people who had passed by without helping the poor wounded man. They thought they were very good and religious; they kept all the rules of the Church; and this poor creature who had been robbed and beaten up was no affair of theirs. He was not their responsibility, so they had passed by on the other side. But Christ said that His disciples must be like the Samaritan who, though a foreigner and a stranger in the land, had compassion on the poor sufferer; tending his wounds and taking him to an inn, spending the night there with him, and paying all his expenses. He made himself entirely responsible for him, though he had never seen him before and, perhaps, would never see him again.

"*Anybody* who is in trouble," said Mr. Elliot, "is our responsibility. That is the law of Christ —Who was always ready to have compassion, whether on a single individual or 'on the multitude'. 'Jesus had compassion on him.' 'Jesus, filled with compassion.' How often we read these words in the Gospels. And it was not only bodily infirmities and sickness that He healed, in His compassion. To the paralyzed man He said: 'Thy sins be forgiven thee,' *before* He told him to 'Arise and walk . . .' because sin is far more terrible than bodily sickness. So terrible is this disease of the soul, that Christ suffered and died on the cross in order that we might be saved from it.

"Your sin may be a secret one; it may be so small and so well hidden that your friends don't notice that there is anything wrong. But little by little, it will spread until it poisons your whole life."

Pauline crouched down behind the people in front of her till she was kneeling on the ground. She was sure that Mr. Elliot must know about her . . . that he was talking directly to her. She was too frightened to pay attention to his closing words.

"Come to Him to-night, and ask Him to heal you. Open the door of your heart to Him; say, Heal my soul, for I have sinned against Thee. Now—while we sing our next hymn: ' It is a thing most wonderful.''

The congregation sang it very softly, swaying slightly in time to the music, as Jamaicans do.

> " I sometimes think about the Cross,
>   And shut my eyes and try to see
> The cruel nails and crown of thorns,
>   And Jesus, crucified for me.
> But even could I see Him die
>   I'd only know a little part
> Of that great love which, like a fire,
>   Is always burning in His heart."

Pauline hardly heard the prayers and the Blessing and the final hymn. Her one thought was to get home quickly and talk to her mother. It wouldn't be easy; Mama would be very angry; but the sooner it was over, the better. She pushed her way through the crowd to where Mama was standing, close to a group of children who seemed very pleased and excited about something. Then she saw that they were all holding hymn-books like her own. The English lady, Mrs. Elliot, had bought several of the books and she was giving them away to the children. Suddenly she caught sight of Pauline.

"Here," she said smiling. "I have just one left for you." Before she had time to think of what she was saying, Pauline replied: "I've got one, thank you," and pulled it out from the front of her dress.

"Good girl! So you bought one for yourself," said the lady, giving her last book to another child.

"How did you get that book, Pauline?" Mama asked sharply. "If someone lent it you, you must give it back at once."

"Why—it's my little orange-girl from the market!" exclaimed Mrs. Elliot, bending down to look into Pauline's face. "You played a nice trick on me this morning! But I suppose it was my own fault, for not finding out what oranges cost here. Everyone laughed at me when they heard I'd paid two shillings for them!"

"No, Mistress—you must be mistaking her for another child," Mama said laughing. "Pauline would never have had the face to ask two shillings for a string of twelve—good though our oranges are, and glad though I'd be of the extra money. *One* shilling she got for our lot."

"Oh well—perhaps I was mistaken, then. It's easy to get confused in a strange country . . . but I thought I recognized the pretty dress with the red and white stripes."

"Besides, Pauline went to the market in the early morning on her way to school," Mama continued, anxious to prove her point. "You wouldn't have been there that soon, Mistress."

"No, that's true; I didn't get there till later on in the morning," Mrs. Elliot agreed.

Pauline twisted her hands together, crushing the book between them. With every word that she allowed them to speak, she was acting a lie. It was true what the missioner had said . . . her soul was diseased; the infection was spreading through her whole life. There was no getting away from it. She had meant to confess to Mama when she got home; but she couldn't—she *couldn't* do it here, with the English lady looking on. It would seem as if she was only sorry because she had been caught out; she would never be able to make them understand.

Owen had woken up and had begun to whimper; and while Mama comforted him, Mrs. Elliot drew Pauline aside.

"Have you 'come home' tonight?" she asked gently.

"Home?" Pauline repeated. "We don't live here, Mistress; our home's further down the hill, quite a step away."

" I meant—have you come home to our Lord? " explained the lady. " Have you opened the door —and asked Him to come in? "

Pauline hesitated, shuffling her feet; then she shook her head.

" Isn't that what you want to do? " asked her friend kindly. Someone had put another record on the gramophone in the car, without switching on the loudspeaker. The music came softly through the warm night air, spicy with the scent of orange trees and lemon trees and many night-scented flowers. Pauline remembered how, like Julie, she had thought the singing was from a choir of angels, coming with the Lord Jesus; and how she had wanted to hide—because she was not ready to meet Him. *Of course* she wanted to open her heart to Him; of course she wanted to " come home ", longed for it more than anything. But how could she dare to meet Him with all these lies between her and Mama—between her and the lady—between her and God?

" I—I'm not ready, yet," she gasped, and wriggled away through the throng to where Mama had joined the neighbours with whom they would walk home.

Chapter 5

CONFESSION

WHEN they reached the house, she got Julie ready for bed while Mama was settling Owen; then she undressed and sat on the edge of her bed, waiting. When her mother came in to tuck her up, she said:

"Mama, I've been very bad to-day. I've done a terrible lot of sins. I didn't go to school at all . . . I stayed at the market all the time. I—I—I made that lady give me two shillings for your oranges . . . and—and I kept one shilling myself—and I bought this book with it. I told you a lie about the money . . . and I told a lie about the embroidery."

It sounded a fearful lot of badness to have done in one day, and she was not surprised to see Mama look—first bewildered, then astonished, then very angry. But she had not expected to see her put her hands over her face and begin to cry. It was dreadful and frightening . . . such a thing had never happened before.

"How could you do it, child?" she sobbed. "What's going to become of you—if you've gone so far already. I can't seem to take it in . . . that you never went to school at all . . . and—d'you mean to tell me it *was* you that tricked the lady into paying too much for the fruit? "

Pauline nodded, then hung her head, speechless with shame.

" And you stood there, bold as brass, and let me say all that to her! Don't you see, you've made me into a liar? Me—that's always struggled to keep straight and live honest, though it's meant going hungry time and time again."

" Still—everyone in the market tries to get as much as they can for their fruit," Pauline protested. " There's nothing so very bad about that, is there? "

" 'Tisn't that," her mother said, drying her eyes. " It's that you caused me to tell Mrs. Elliot what wasn't true. That's not like a child telling fibs— though I've brought you up to tell the truth, and it's a shock to find that you can be so sly; but for me—a grown woman—to tell a barefaced lie to a lady who trusted me, that's something I can't bear to think of."

" But you *thought* it was the truth, then—so you *weren't* telling a lie," argued Pauline.

" It's all in the family," sighed her mother, who was beginning to get a little muddled. " What with what's true and what isn't, I don't know if I'm coming or going, and that's a fact. But are you really sorry, child? "

"Oh yes, Mama. Very, very sorry."

"And have you asked the Lord to forgive you?"

Pauline's tears had begun to flow again. "Not yet," she whispered. "I didn't seem able to say my prayers—till I'd told you."

Mrs. Cole was tired and perplexed. It had been a great shock to her to learn that Pauline had been able to deceive her so easily. Otherwise she might have realized that her daughter needed help and advice, and that this might prove to be a turning-point in her life.

"Well, since you've owned up in the end, I'll say no more at present," she said, getting up. "Kneel down and say your prayers—and then try and get to sleep." After she had gone, Pauline knelt by her bed for a long time, so exhausted with crying that she could neither feel nor think. She stumbled through the Our Father, and got into bed. But just before she fell asleep, she murmured: "Lord—be merciful—to me—a sinner."

Mama was very silent at breakfast next morning, as if she were turning over something in her mind. Pauline hoped that she was going to be allowed to set out for school without any more being said about her misdoings; but just as she was starting, Mama called her back.

"I've been thinking about what happened yesterday," she said. "And I've reckoned out that we've got to do our best to put things right. What you did wrong is between you and the Lord, and

D

if you've said you're sorry, you must trust in His mercy to forgive you. But the Bible says we've got to make things right with other people, too; so—first, you're going to own up to Teacher about playing truant yesterday; you're not to let her go thinking I kept you at home. Next—when school's over, you're to go to the Rectory where Mrs. Elliot is stopping. You'll tell her the truth—just tell her what happened—and you'll give her this money—" here Mama produced a sixpence and six coppers from a tin box on the table "—and tell her, from me, that I didn't know nothing about it when she spoke to us yesterday."

Pauline began to cry. "No, Mama, no—please!" she begged. "I'll own up to Teacher . . . but I *can't* go to the Rectory and tell all that to the lady."

"That's what you're going to do," Mama said quietly. "You wronged your teacher by not turning up at school; and you wronged Mrs. Elliot when you swindled her. Oh, I don't reckon a shilling, one way or the other, means much to her, but wrong's wrong, whether you do someone out of a shilling or out of a pound. And most of all, you've wronged me, your mother, by trying to do me out of a shilling, and—what's a lot worse—by making me look a liar to that nice kind lady. Now, that's all got to be put right, and I don't want to see you back here till you can tell me it's done."

Pauline's heart was heavy as she walked slowly

down the track, instead of running and skipping
as she usually did. On most mornings she loved
the walk to school and took pleasure in all she saw;
the small lizards sunning themselves on the red
sun-baked earth; the brilliant humming-birds
hovering over the flowering bushes, dipping their
long beaks into the honey-laden blossoms; the wild
canaries and the little striped birds called banana-
quits which flew across the path in front of her.
But to-day she could only think of the dreaded
tasks which lay ahead. She could not see to the
end of the day: she was unable to imagine that
there could be an ending to a day which was to
contain such appalling difficulties. The interview
with Teacher would be bad enough, though that—
at least—was within the scope of her imagination.
It was quite usual for children to be absent from
school, generally because their parents needed
needed them at home, or to make extra money by
doing seasonal work in the fields. Some of the
boys and girls only pretended that this had been
the reason; especially in the case of the boys, who
would go off fishing for the day, cooking their
" catch " on sticks over a fire by the side of the pool.

Pauline had been more regular in attendance
than most, Mama had seen to that, and Teacher
would be shocked and disappointed to learn that
she had stayed away with no excuse. But far, far
worse would be her confession to the Mission lady.
Even the prospect of going up the Rectory drive,

ringing the front-door bell and asking for Mrs.
Elliot made her feel quite cold inside. And—if
Archdeacon should be there! The very thought
made her long for an earthquake, a really bad one,
so that the ground might open and swallow her
up. There was not a child in the parish who did
not know and love the Archdeacon. They all
clustered around him when he came out to the
churchyard after service, or when he paid one of
his frequent informal visits to the school. But
Pauline felt that she would gladly die rather than
that he should come to hear of her misdeeds.

Luckily, she arrived early at school, and was
able to make her confession to Teacher privately
instead of in front of the whole class. Teacher
seemed more sorry than angry, and she made
Pauline feel even sorrier than she had been before.

"You see, it isn't fair on Mama to miss your
lessons," she explained. "You could be helping
her at home, even, before long, going out to work
and bringing home some money to her. But instead of letting you work for wages, she sends you
here to get educated. With education, you will
have a happier and more interesting life; but you
are also fitting yourself for a better job than you
could have if you were uneducated. You'd like to
be able to help Mama when you are older,
wouldn't you? And you can't do that unless you
get a good job."

"Yes, Teacher." Pauline said what she thought

was expected of her—and because it was easier to agree than to disagree. But actually she could not see how the lessons she was made to learn could help her to get a job when she left school.

"When you miss a day at school, you are being unfair to me, too," Teacher went on. "You see, *I* have to turn up here every morning, whether I feel like it or not. What would you say if you came all the way to school one morning and found there was no Teacher?"

Privately, Pauline thought it would be quite a nice surprise. It would mean an unexpected holiday . . . unless Miss Benyon, the Headmistress, set them some sums on the blackboard or made them learn poetry by heart, or something. It would be a change, anyway. However, it wouldn't have been polite to say this out loud, and the ringing of the school bell brought the lecture to an end.

During recess, she gave her lunch-money to another girl and asked her to bring her a cake and an "icicle" from the bakery, as she wanted to do some extra work on her embroidery. Her entry for the competition was a tablecloth with a border worked with different Jamaican flowers, and there was a large bouquet of the flowers in each corner. She loved needlework, it was by far her best subject, and many people thought that she stood a good chance of winning the first prize this year. Her chief rivals were Alice Wilson and Jennifer

Haynes, both of whom worked so beautifully that Pauline felt less hopeful for her own chances every time she looked at their entries. Alice's stitching was finer and more exquisitely worked than that of the other two, added to which she was a quick and tireless worker. If the exhibits were to be judged by the actual quality of the stitching and by the amount of work put into it, Alice's bedspread could not fail to win. Jennifer had a flair for designing and a good eye for colour, and there were plenty of people who thought that her set of six place-mats was sure to get the prize. The mats were being carried out entirely in appliqué-work, and the design for each represented a different scene in the market.

Pauline's ideas were not so dashingly original as Jennifer's, and she had not Alice's skill as an embroideress. Nevertheless, her border and corner-bouquets had a delicate charm of their own. Lately, though, she had been feeling doubtful as to whether the colours were sufficiently striking; and it had been Teacher's suggestion that she should unpick the pale-blue flowers and substitute some poinsettias—the large scarlet star-shaped flowers which grow so freely in Jamaica. Teacher had had to send away for the scarlet silk, and Pauline's work had been held up for lack of it. It had been due to arrive on the previous day, and she would have been able to start work on the vivid red flowers if she had not stayed away from school.

She now went to find Teacher to ask her for the silk, refusing to join in the games which some of the others were organizing in the playground. Several of them were playing a simplified form of baseball, which is rather like the English game of rounders. Others were playing "Chevy Chase", a game rather similar to "Fox and Geese"; all except one player were in a file, each with his arms round the one in front, and this file twisted and turned to prevent the single player from catching the one at the "tail" of the file.

Some of the children had already started to eat the lunches they had bought at the bakery, while little boys fetched drinking-water from the "catchments". These are high circular concrete tanks storing rain-water, with a tap at the base. As the boys were apt to be rough with the taps, only the teachers were allowed to use them; the children had a light ladder which reached to the top of the tank. A boy would climb the ladder and let down a home-made "bucket", which was really a tin with a long string attached; and in this he would haul up enough drinking-water for himself and his friends.

While all this activity was going on in the playground, the girls who were anxious to get on with their sewing sat on the wooden steps leading to the raised floor of the classroom. The classroom had only three walls, one side being left open, because in that hot climate it is necessary to let in as much

air as possible.   Before going to fetch the new silk,
Pauline had reserved a place for herself next to
Alice by putting her sewing, wrapped in a white
cloth, on the step beside her friend.

Teacher looked surprised when Pauline asked
her for the silk. " I left it on your desk yesterday,"
she said.   " Of course I didn't know that you
wouldn't be coming, and I thought no more about
it.   I expect someone put it inside the desk for
you."

Pauline ran back to look; but even after turning out all the contents of the desk, no red silk was
to be seen.   She went back to Teacher, who came
herself to help in the search, saying that it *must*
be there.   Pauline went to ask the sewing-party if
they had seen it; but though some of them remembered having noticed the paper packet lying on her
desk the day before, nobody knew what had happened to it.

" What can I do, Teacher? " Pauline was nearly
crying.   " I can't get on without it . . . I've already done all but the poinsettia flowers—and
there's such a lot of those   And there's only two
weeks to the competition."

Teacher was kind and sympathetic, though she
felt bound to point out that this would never have
happened if Pauline had not stayed away from
school.

" I'd send away for some more," she said,
" though it's a great waste of money; those em-

broidery silks are expensive. But I'm sure it wouldn't be here in time for you to work all those flowers before the competition."

"What *am* I to do, then?" gulped Pauline, unfolding the tablecloth and gazing mournfully at the finished flowers, and leaves, and at the spaces left for the poinsettias. "It was going to be so lovely. I wanted it to be so lovely."

"Yes, it's a charming design, and you've put a lot of good work into it," Teacher said, looking as if she felt just as disappointed as Pauline, "but I'm afraid there's nothing for you to do but to go back to your first idea—before we thought of the poinsettias. Those pale-blue flowers will look very pretty, really."

"I shan't like it a bit that way, now," Pauline muttered. "It'll all be dull and pale . . . there's no life in it, without a bit of scarlet."

"I don't see what we can do about it, though." Teacher looked at the clock. She had not eaten her lunch yet, and in a minute or two the bell would ring for classes to start again. But she felt very sorry for Pauline, who looked so unhappy, she didn't like to leave her alone.

When the class reassembled and all the boys and girls were sitting with their slates ready in front of them, their bare feet curled round the legs of the chairs, Teacher asked if anyone had found the missing packet of embroidery silk; and when school was over for the day, she helped Pauline to look through the contents of her desk all over again; but all without success.

"You know, Pauline, you are dreadfully untidy," she sighed, shaking her head over the muddle inside the desk. "You really must try to be more methodical and to keep things in their proper places. You're so careless and forgetful, too; I'm not surprised that you're always losing things."

This rebuke reminded Pauline that they had not yet looked to see if the packet of silk had found its way into the Lost Property cupboard. This was where the teachers put any article found lying about after the children had gone home. A halfpenny fine had to be paid before anything could be claimed; Pauline was one of the worst offenders, and her carelessness often cost her a halfpenny out of her lunch-money. But there was no red silk in the cupboard, and they had to resign themselves to the sad fact that the packet must have been accidentally swept up and thrown away when the room was cleaned.

Pauline had been so distressed about her embroidery, she completely forgot her other troubles until she was leaving the school building. Then it all came back with a rush; the terrifying fact that she must not go home till she had seen Mrs. Elliot. It seemed too much to bear after the disappoinment she had had, and her feet dragged as she crossed the playground to the school entrance. Her only hope lay in the possibility of Mrs. Elliot being out for the day. Then she could just leave the money, and a message explaining about it, with Lilah, Archdeacon's maid; and Mama would surely let her off going there again to make her confession.

To her surprise, Mark Bailey was waiting for her outside the school gate. He seemed to want to tell her something without knowing how to begin. They walked down to the street together in silence for a few minutes; then she asked shyly: "Did you —get away all right, yesterday?"

"Yes," he replied. "They didn't follow me for long; they gave up, after a while." Then he added: "Thank you—for giving me the warning. They'd have got me, *and* Granny's supper, if it hadn't been for you."

"If that had happened, would your Granny have had nothing to eat?" Pauline asked, wide-eyed.

"No supper, and no breakfast, either," was the reply. "She has to lie in bed all day . . . she can't get up because her legs are paralyzed. Mama brings her something at midday, though it's a long way to go. And she gives me the basket, soon as I get home from school, with something for supper and for our breakfast the next morning."

"Do you sleep there, then?" asked Pauline. He nodded again. "Someone has to sleep with her, in case she wants anything in the night. The other room's let to a woman who goes out to work all day; she washes Granny and makes the bed before she goes, but she doesn't like being disturbed at night, and she doesn't do any cooking."

"So your Granny's alone all day?"

"Except when Mama comes; and she hasn't time to stay long. Granny loves having visitors more than anything," he added awkwardly. "She—she'd like to see *you*. She said—to thank you—about yesterday."

Pauline's heart ached for the lonely old woman who had to be in bed all day; but she didn't think she'd ever have the courage to go and see her. However, she murmured something polite about "maybe, some day . . .". And then, Mark said: "I wanted to do something for you, sort of in return. I don't know if it's any use, but—about that embroidery silk you've lost . . ."

"Yes—yes—what is it? D'you know where it is?"

"I'm not sure. But yesterday, I saw Jennifer Haynes pick up something from off your desk—I *think* it was your desk—and put it in her bag, when everyone was leaving. I didn't think anything at the time, it might have been something she'd just put down there for a minute; but then, when Teacher asked us all about it, I remembered——"

Pauline stood still, and clutched his arm.

"But—she never said——"

"I know," he agreed. "I was waiting and waiting for her to say something about it—but never a word!"

"Perhaps—but she *couldn't* have—it isn't as if she needed it for her own work," murmured Pauline. She wouldn't want that colour; and—and—*why* should she play such a dirty trick?"

"She might have a reason," he whispered. "Plenty of folks is saying you and she have an even chance for the competition. Maybe—she thought yours would be too pretty with the red flowers in it . . . and that you'd get ahead of her."

Chapter 6

A NEW FRIEND

MRS. ELLIOT was resting in the Rectory garden, in the shade of a great mahogany tree. She had visited several schools during the hottest time of the day, and had afterwards given an address at a special meeting for women in the Church Hall; so she was glad to relax now in the comfortable aluminium-and-canvas chair. Lilah had been glad to put out this chair, which was as good as a bed. "The people of Archdeacon's last parish gave it him when he left there," she said. "But it's never been used, from that day to this! You'd think a man who works as hard as he does would be glad of a rest now and then; but you never see Archdeacon take his ease—not till he goes to his bed at night! And that's not till late—and he's up early in the morning, too"!

It was pleasant to lie and watch the butterflies—and the humming-birds, which were no bigger than butterflies; to feast her eyes on the blaze of colour, and to remember that this was February. She had counted ten different kinds of begonias in

full flower, and as many different orchids, and
there were hibiscus and bougainvillea, big red lilies
and pink lilies, great bushes of poinsettia, and of
deturah, that huge white trumpet-shaped flower
with the heavy sweet scent. Lilah had brought
her a glass of iced lemonade made from the enormous lemons which grew on a tree nearby.

Seeing the girl approaching her again. Mrs.
Ellliot thought she had come to fetch the empty
glass; but Lilah fidgeted and hesitated, and finally
told her that there was a little girl at the door, asking for the Missioner's wife.

"I tell her you're resting, Mistress; but she just
keep' on standing there, and won't go till she's seen
you."

"Do you know who she is, Lilah?" asked
Mrs. Elliot, preparing to get up and go to the
house.

"Sure, I know her. Now—don't you disturb
yourself, Missis; I'll bring her right here, if you're
willing to see her. I'd have sent her packing, only
that I know her mother is a good respectable
woman. She's bringing up her pickneys well, for
all she's so poor—and her husband dead and
gone."

Mrs. Elliot had already learnt that "pickney"
was the Jamaican word for a child—or piccaninny;
and she willingly agreed for this one to be brought
to her.

To someone new to Jamaica, it is not always

easy to distinguish one "pickney" from another; but Mrs. Elliot immediately recognized in Pauline the little orange-seller of the market—who had turned up at the Mission service the night before, with a hymn-book she had bought for herself.

"Well, my dear, what can I do for you—Pauline —isn't that your name?" she asked kindly. But Pauline stood on her right leg, rubbing her left foot up and down it, as was her habit when embarrassed.

"Well, now—you've come all the way to see me; surely you've got something to say?" Mrs. Elliot urged her. "Was it perhaps something about the service last night that you wanted to ask me?"

She hoped that the girl had come to say she wanted to ask Christ to come into her heart . . . but at the question about the service Pauline shook her head. Then, without any warning, huge tears welled up in her big dark eyes and began to run down her little black face; and suddenly she took something from the palm-leaf she was carrying and held it out to the Englishwoman. It was something screwed into a piece of paper; Mrs. Elliot took it from her, opened it, and saw—to her surprise—six pennies and a sixpence.

"What's this for, Pauline?" she asked. "Why are you bringing me money?"

"It's—it's yours!" gasped Pauline. "Mama said—to bring it to you—'cause I'd made her into a liar . . and she's not one, really. Mama never tells no lies."

" I'm sure she doesn't," Mrs. Elliot agreed, wondering how she was ever to get to the bottom of this mystery, and wishing that the Archdeacon had been there. " Tell me why you think you made your Mama into a liar," she continued gently. " Or would you like to wait here till Archdeacon comes home, and explain it to him? "

" Oh no—*no!* " Pauline almost shrieked the words, and seized Mrs. Elliot's arm with her skinny little hands. " Don't you tell him, Missis! Please, *please* don't tell him! "

" I won't tell him anything you ask me not to," promised the puzzled lady. " But—*what* is it that I'm not to tell him? "

" About—what I done," whispered the girl.

" Could you tell me from the beginning, do you think? "

Pauline wrinkled her forehead, trying to remember what the beginning had been. " Mama sent me to market with the oranges, on the way to school," she found at last. " Because she was short this week . . . and she said—not less than ninepence—and a shilling if you can   And—it was so good at the market . . . I thought I'd miss school and stay there all day.   And—and—I saw you being kind to the poor donkey, and I asked you two shillings, just to see. And you never laughed, you paid up the two shillings. And I put one in

E

this bag for Mama—and—and—I kept the other. And I went back to the stalls and walked up and down, but I couldn't settle, so I went out— and there was Judith Holmes selling books for a shilling——" She broke off and hung her head.

"So that's how you came to have a hymn-book of your own? And your mother knew nothing about all this?"

Pauline shook her head. "When she said—it wasn't me, the girl who sold you the oranges, she thought she was telling the truth. She didn't know she was being a liar."

It all seemed to be out now, and Pauline drew a deep breath.

"And afterwards—you felt very sorry?" prompted Mrs. Elliot.

"Oh yes! I felt terrible sorry."

"And when did you begin to feel so terribly sorry?"

"It was last night—at the Mission. If the sing-ing had *really* been angels, and the Lord was com-ing—I wouldn't have been able to meet Him. And after—there was that hymn——" Pauline lowered her voice; "I sometimes think about the Cross . . . and shut my eyes." She closed her eyes, and was silent for a minute.

"It seemed so cruel," she whispered then. "Him—hanging there . . . and it seemed—as if it was my fault."

"'And Jesus crucified for me.' Yes, your fault and my fault, because of our sinfulness . . . to save us from our sins. It must have hurt so much to be crucified. It's dreadful to hurt Him still more, isn't it? And what would hurt Him most of all is for us to refuse to be saved from sin, when He paid so much to save us."

Pauline was crying again. "I wish I hadn't done any sins!" she wailed. "I wish I hadn't hurt Him."

"Did you tell Him that, when you said your prayers last night?" asked the Englishwoman.

The reply came so low that she could hardly hear it.

"I said—Lord—be merciful to me—a sinner."

"And do you know for certain that He has had mercy on you? Has He come into your heart? Are you His very own, now?"

"I don't know. I didn't ask nothing else . . . just for mercy."

"Just for mercy!" repeated Mrs. Elliot gently. "That should cover everything; and it could mean that you want to belong to Him. All the same, I expect He'd like to hear you say it."

Together they knelt down on the lawn of Bahama grass, which is more like prickly little leaves than our grass; and Mrs. Elliot said the words for Pauline, who repeated them after her.

"Lord, have mercy upon me, a sinner. Receive

me as Thy child, O Lord, and defend me with Thy Heavenly Grace, and bring me to Thy everlasting Kingdom."

Pauline knew that she ought to be getting home, but she lingered in the garden, trying to make up her mind to ask a question.

"Did you ever see the donkey again? " she got out at last.

"What donkey? "

"The one in the market. He was very thin, and he had a sore mouth—and you had compassion on him."

As she spoke, something in the tone of her voice and the expression on her face touched her kind friend.

"You are fond of animals? " she asked.

"Oh yes, Mistress. But they are often so sad, and nobody seems to care." Pauline's eyes filled with tears again as she continued, as if to herself:

"And some of the little children . . . and old people . . ." She couldn't explain what she meant, but Mrs. Elliot looked as if she understood.

"It's like a load pressing on your heart, isn't it? You long to help, but there are so many of them, you don't know where to begin."

"That's just it! " Pauline said eagerly. "It's so awful to think of them all—I try *not* to think about it——"

" No, don't shut your heart to the sufferings of others," Mrs. Elliot said quickly. " Don't quench your feeling of compassion; it has been given you by our Lord, so that you may use it for His sake. You can't help all the poor animals, but help them whenever you get the chance; you can't help all the neglected children, but you may know one or two who you can comfort with your kindness and love. You can't help all the poor old people, but maybe there is a lonely old woman somewhere whose life would be made happier if you went to visit her now and then."

" Like Mark's Granny," remembered Pauline. " He wants me to go and see her; she's in bed all day, and ever so lonely."

" Well, there's somewhere for you to start right away," Mrs. Elliot said as they walked back to the house together. " Now that you belong to our Lord, you'll find He will give you plenty to do for Him. Remember that He said: ' Inasmuch as ye have done it to these, ye have done it unto Me.' "

Before saying goodbye, she asked Pauline to come into the Rectory for a moment, and took her to a room where there was an upright piano. Sitting at the piano, she began to play and sing:

" Save me from my sin, Lord.
    Put Thy power within, Lord.
    Take me as I am, Lord,
    And make me all Thine own.
    Keep me day by day . . ."

When she had finished the verse, she made Pauline sing it with her, and told her to use it as a prayer.

"And give my love to your mother," she added. "And thank her, for me, for sending you here to-day. And—don't forget to tell her of your decision."

Pauline sang the verse through several times on the way home, until she was sure she would not forget it. She hurried along, for she no longer felt tired and her heart was light. Her mother was watching out for her anxiously. She knew that she had set a hard task before her little daughter, and had been remembering her all day and praying for her. She had truly meant to do what was best for the girl, but, during the day, she wondered whether she had not been too intent on justifying herself—at Pauline's expense. When she saw her child's radiant face and heard everything that had happened at the Rectory, she sat on the bed and took Pauline on her lap as if she had been a baby.

"Now I thank the Lord!" she explained. "Now that you belong to him, I don't need to be anxious about you any more!" She made Pauline repeat over and over again what the Missioner's wife had said, especially the message to herself. That was a happy evening. Mama prepared a special supper, and they had sweet potatoes and fried ackees and cho-cho (a kind of root vegetable) with the usual rice-and-peas.

It was not till Pauline was getting into bed that she remembered the blow about the competition needlework, and the dreadful suspicion about Jennifer Haynes. She called Mama and told her all about it, explaining that if the missing material did not turn up she would have to alter the design all over again.

"And that won't be nearly so pretty," she moaned. "I'll be nowhere near winning if I have to do it that way. But if that girl has taken it, I'll get it from her if I have to tear all her things in pieces to find it! *And* I'll pay her out for it, too."

"And that'll be a fine way to act, on your first day as a disciple of the Lord!" retorted her mother. "You be careful, Pauline child, and remember it's a serious matter—accusing someone of pinching what isn't theirs."

"But the girls at school are always pinching each other's things, Mama; you know they are. More than half the quarrels are over that."

"You don't know for certain she took it," argued her mother. "You've only one person's word for it . . . and Mark Bailey might have made a mistake. You said yourself that his desk is nowhere near your own; he might easily have mistaken another for it. Or she might have set something of her own down there for a moment, and taken it up again."

"She might have—but I don't think she did," muttered Pauline. "She's just the sort who'd play a mean trick like that—especially if it helped her to win the competition. It's a money prize, you know; and I've noticed Jennifer's always short of money."

Mrs. Cole was silent for a few minutes, thinking this over.

"Even if Jennifer did this bad thing," she said then, "I want you to promise me not to bear malice. The Lord said we are to forgive those who wrong us, and be good to those who persecute us. That's not just a way of speaking; it's a real solid thing He has told us to do. Don't you go and disappoint Him, now—the very first time you're tested."

Pauline promised to try and remember what her mother had said; but she didn't see how she was ever going to be able to put it into practice.

Chapter 7

JENNIFER

SHE got to school early next morning, and went up to Jennifer as soon as she arrived.

"I want my embroidery silk, please, Jennifer," she said. "You know, the scarlet silk Teacher left on my desk, day before yesterday."

"I'm afraid I don't know what you're talking about." Jennifer spoke contemptuously, and her half-smile was insolent. She was a Jamaican of mixed descent, with golden eyes and a skin the colour of coffee and cream. She would have been extremely pretty if her expression had been happier and more straightforward. Her gaze, now, flickered round the room; she very seldom looked directly at the person to whom she was speaking.

"Teacher left it right here," Pauline repeated, as patiently as she could. "And you—someone saw you take something off my desk——"

"I wouldn't dream of touching your desk—or anything of yours!" was the rude retort. "Besides —why should I be wanting your silk? I've plenty of my own, thanks."

She unwrapped her own work as she spoke, and

73

displayed her set of mats in all their perfection. Pauline was always attracted by what was beautiful, and she gazed with wistful admiration at the bold colourful designs. Their colouring was vivid, strikingly so; but no scarlet silk had been used in the work, nor would any be needed.

"Well, I'm sorry," she said at last. "I suppose Mark—I suppose there must have been a mistake."

"What's the matter, Paulie?" Alice asked kindly. "Haven't you found that silk yet?"

"No," Pauline sighed. "Must have got thrown away by mistake, I guess. I'll—I'll just have to do without."

"Cheer up, Pauline!" Teacher had entered the classroom, unnoticed by the three girls. "I think you may be able to have the red flowers in your embroidery after all. A friend of mine is going to Kingston tomorrow, and I've asked her to bring back another supply of the silk for you. She'll get back late tomorrow evening, but you'll have it by the next morning."

"Oh Teacher—thank you! How lovely!" The girl's eyes shone, but her face clouded over again when she considered what the delay would mean to her work.

"But will I ever get it done in time for the competition?" she asked dolefully.

"I really believe you will, if you set your mind to it. Now, get into your places; the bell's just going to ring."

"All the same, I hate that nasty Jennifer!"
Pauline whispered to Alice during recess. "Did
you see how sour she looked when she heard I'd
have my silk after all? I'm sure she'd play me a
dirty trick if she got the chance."

"Maybe we'd be nasty too, if we were in her
shoes," Alice said mildly. "I wouldn't like to be
her, I know that!"

"Why? What's wrong with her?"

"Well, her parents are dead, you know; and her
elder brother and his wife give her a home . . .
but it's not much of a home. Joe Haynes is a
rough type, and his wife grudges every bite Jennifer eats. Many a day she goes without lunch,
'cause she's got nothing to pay the bakery."

Pauline glanced at Jennifer who sat, as usual,
apart from the other girls, sewing as if her life
depended on it. One ought to pity a girl who had
an unhappy home and no parents; but Jennifer
was so haughty and stuck up, and had such a horrid
sneering way with her; it was impossible to feel
sorry for her.

Seeing that Mark Bailey had dropped out of the
game of baseball, Pauline decided to go and talk
to him. There was nothing more that she could
do with her work, at present; she had merely been
touching up the outlined design for the poinsettia
flowers, now that she knew she was going to be able
to complete them. Leaving her embroidery in
Alice's charge, she ran across the playground to

where Mark was standing. "D'you think your Granny would really like me to come and see her?" she asked shyly.

"Like it? Why—she'd be as pleased as pleased!" he exclaimed gratefully. "When could you come?"

"Would Saturday be a good time?" she suggested. "I can't come this evening—there's the big Mission service in the Church here, and Mama says I may go if I've finished my home duties in time."

"Saturday will do fine," Mark told her. "I'll tell Granny, so as she'll be looking forward to it. She gets awful lonesome during the daytime."

Although Pauline was in a hurry to get home so as to be ready in time to go to the service, she went a considerable distance out of her way in order to follow Jennifer, who lived some way out on the opposite side of the town from where Pauline's own house was. Her interest in the other girl had been aroused, and she felt curious about her; not through sympathy . . . rather through a kind of morbid fascination in one who she instinctively felt to be her enemy. She kept well out of sight while Jennifer sauntered through the streets; but once clear of the town, it was difficult to keep pace with her without being seen. Jennifer walked fast, and soon turned off the road and ascended the hillside by a narrow track. Leaving this, she struck out along a mere thread of a path which was no more than a goat-walk; no wheeled vehicle had ever been that way. Pauline had to keep her in sight as best she could, taking cover where possible behind the occasional bushes and stunted trees.

Now that she believed herself to be alone, Jennifer walked more slowly, pausing from time to time as if she were in no hurry to get home. Her face was no longer haughty and sneering; she looked sulky and depressed . . . "like someone who has never known what it was to have something nice to look forward to—" . . . that was how Pauline put it to herself. But suddenly her expression changed, making her into an entirely different person. The sulkiness vanished and the sadness too, to be replaced by a look of delighted happiness. Pauline peered cautiously from her hiding-place to see what had caused the transformation, and in a moment she understood. Growing beside the path was a bush, covered with small crimson flowers; and over and among these flowers, three—four . . . no, five . . six—at least *eight* humming-birds were fluttering and hovering, pausing for a second to dip their beaks into the blossoms, then fluttering on—always moving. With their plumage of bright blue and emerald green, they were like a moving display of brilliant jewels, and all this beauty and gaiety and light were reflected on Jennifer's face, as she gazed and gazed. Now Pauline understood why there was always something special about Jennifer's embroidery designs, as with the pictures she painted in Art class. Pauline, realized in her heart—she could never have put it into words—that beauty was to Jennifer what food and drink are to other people; and that it gave her perhaps the only happiness she ever knew.

But this moment of ecstasy was short-lived. From somewhere out of Pauline's range of vision a harsh voice called Jennifer's name, and immediately her face became hard and sullen as before. She walked on, scowling and dragging her feet; then Pauline heard the same voice exclaim:

"Hurry yourself, you idle trash! Get to your work quick, or there'll be no supper for you . . . and I know that's all you care about!"

There was the sound of a stinging slap; then a man's voice joined in the scolding, and Pauline heard a half-suppressed cry, as if Jennifer had received a heavier blow. The voices became more indistinct, so the speakers must have gone indoors. Slowly and cautiously, Pauline crept out from behind the clump of croton bushes; crawled on hands and knees until, round a bend of the hillside, she saw a wooden shack with a tin roof. It consisted of one room only, and was the loneliest, dreariest-looking place she had ever seen. There were no fruit-trees, no vegetable patch; no goat and no chickens; just this miserable hut standing by itself on the wild hillside. Bunches of split palm-leaves, tied ready for plaiting, lay on the ground outside the door. These were for weaving hats and baskets, carrier-bags and mats, and must be the "work" to which Jennifer had been summoned: there could be nothing else for her to do in this derelict place. There was a clamour of angry voices inside the hut; it sounded as if the flimsy walls might burst at any moment. Pauline turned and ran down the path, ran and ran until she was out of earshot. Then she paused for breath; but there was a dreadful feeling inside her—the same feeling that she had about ill-treated animals and unhappy children and lonely old people. She began to run again, very fast so as to escape from her thoughts, because she didn't want to have to think of Jennifer, of all people, in that particular way.

Chapter 8

"SOMEONE HAS TAKEN IT!"

"I'VE put your sewing in your desk," Alice said next morning. "You never came back for it after recess yesterday, you bad girl! And when I looked for you after school, you'd already left; so I took it home with mine for the night."

"Oh Alice—you are good! I wish I wasn't so forgetful," sighed Pauline. She knew she deserved to lose her things and have them get spoilt; Teacher had told her so again and again, and so had Mama. Her work had been quite safe with Alice, though; Alice was the most trustworthy girl in the school, and her home was so clean and neat: the precious table-cloth had been better off there than in the untidy confusion of its owner's desk. To-morrow she would be able to get to work on it again; but in the meantime, while she was waiting for the new supply of silk, it was nice to join in a game of Chevy Chase for a change, during recess. It was so long since she had been able to spare the time for games, and there would certainly be no more playing for her till after the competition.

She came in to class hot and breathless, and was

not quite so attentive as she should have been.
Teacher had to speak quite sharply to her, and
after that Pauline tried hard to concentrate. She
didn't want to behave badly in class when Teacher
had been so kind, getting the sewing materials for
her twice over. When it came, she would have to
work, harder than ever in her life before, to get
finished in time for the competition. But she'd
manage it somehow—if only to show Teacher how
grateful she was.

But, when school was breaking up: "Alice!"
she called, her voice sharp with anxiety. "Alice
—I thought you said you'd put the sewing in my
desk?"

"Yes—and I did put it there, too." Alice was
busy gathering up her own belongings. "Look
again, you untidy child! You've probably buried
it under a lot of rubbish."

"It's *not* here, I tell you. Alice—you *must* help
me find it. I suppose you put it in another desk by
mistake."

In her desperation, Pauline had started throwing
up the lids of all the desks near her own, and
rummaging in one after the other; but now
their owners came back and began to protest.
One girl gave her a spiteful pinch, another
pulled her hair, and in a few minutes a fight
had started.

"Stop it! Stop it, instantly—every one of you."
Teacher's voice was cold and stern. She had been

F

trying to put a stop to these fights among the girls, but they still occurred far too often, and were usually the result of loss of property.

"Now—what is it about this time?" she asked, when order had been restored. Several people tried to speak at once, but she held up her hand.

"One at a time, please. Pauline? You've *lost* your competition embroidery? My dear child— you're hopeless! Do you *never* keep anything in its right place?"

There was a confused babble of explanation, out of which Teacher gathered the main facts: that Pauline had left her work lying about, as usual, and that Alice had kept it for her overnight and put it in her desk this morning.

"And it's not there now? Alice, you're sure you put it in Pauline's desk, not in someone else's by mistake? Well, then, Pauline, you probably took it out some time during the day, and left it lying around somewhere."

"Really and truly I didn't Teacher. I haven't seen it since yesterday." She hesitated, then added in a low voice: "Someone's taken it out of my desk; and I know who did it, too!"

"Now listen, Pauline." Teacher's voice was icy. "You're always losing your possessions, and I'm sick and tired of hearing you say that other people have taken them. I will not have you accusing your schoolfellows of theft every time you've been untidy and careless and forgetful. Even if somebody *had* taken it, you'd only have yourself to blame; and I don't want to hear another word about it."

Pauline was too angry to cry, but her head throbbed and ached, and her legs felt so heavy she could hardly get herself home. And the day had started so happily; the evening before she had been at that wonderful Mission service at the Church. She had heard Mr. Elliot preach, and had joined in the glorious singing. Mrs. Elliot had spoken to her in the Church porch after the service . . . had actually told Pauline to come and see her whenever she liked. And now everything was black and miserable. She couldn't even pray.

Mama was no more sympathetic than Teacher had been; in fact, she was even more indignant with Pauline, partly because of her own intense disappointment. Of course, the embroidery would turn up some time: Pauline had simply left it lying around, and with her usual heedlessness had forgotten where she had put it. But it might have got soiled or even torn; and in any case it couldn't now be finished in time.

"I don't know what's to be done with you, Pauline," she complained. "It isn't as if you didn't mind . . . you were crazy about that competition. But even that didn't make you careful."

"But Mama, I gave it to Alice to take care of, it was safe enough with her. I know I forgot to get it back from her . . . but she put it in my desk. And I *know* someone's stolen it! I'm as certain of that as I am of anything."

"According to you, everything's always been stolen," her mother said wearily.

"This time, I'm sure of it. It's that hateful Jennifer; she wouldn't stop at anything."

"I won't have that wicked talk in my house," Mama said severely. "You're far too ready to think badly of others. Don't you know that every unkind thought is like a great black cloud between you and the Lord? How can you expect to get close to Him when your heart is chock-full of hatred and suspicion?"

Pauline knew that her mother was right. She found it very difficult to pray, and God seemed to be a long way off. Yet—would He really expect her to forgive, if Jennifer had done this mean thing?

When Teacher gave her the red silk next morning, saying: "I suppose this is no use to you now? Still, you'd better take it, just in case . . ." Pauline kept her eyes on Jennifer's face. But Jennifer was absorbed in cleaning her slate; she never even looked up, and it was impossible to know what she was thinking.

During recess, Mark reminded Pauline of the promised visit to his Granny which had been arranged for the following day.

"I'm not sure that I'll come, after all," she said listlessly. "I feel so bad about my competition work, I'll not be very cheerful company. Maybe we'd best leave it till later."

The boy's face fell. "She'll be ever so disappointed," he said. "If you knew how she's been counting on it . . . I know you're downhearted, and I shouldn't bother you; but—I shan't know how to tell her you're not coming after all."

His deep distress, for the sake of another, touched Pauline's heart, even through her own trouble. If Mark could look like this at the thought of giving pain to his Granny, what would the old lady feel herself when he told her that she was not to have a visitor after all?

"I'll come," she said, trying to smile. "Will some time in the afternoon be right? I have to do Mama's shopping for her on Saturday mornings. And will you meet me at that same place near the main road, and show me the way?"

Chapter 9

PAULINE GOES VISITING

SHE gathered some wild flowers on her way to meet Mark; "Spanish Needle", and "Four-o'clock"—so-called because it opens only at that time of the day; rose-coloured hibiscus which the country children call "Shoe-black", because the petals are good for putting a shine on leather shoes.

Mark was waiting for her, and she felt cheered by the sight of his happy face. There was a special sort of joy, she was discovering, in bringing comfort to those in need. How happy Jesus must have been—healing the sick, cheering those who were sad, giving His life for others. The thought that she was helping, even a very little, with His work, gave her a warm safe feeling . . . as if she were walking hand in hand with One Who knew the way.

Old Mrs. Bailey lived in a two-roomed house which, like most Jamaican houses, large or small, was built of "Spanish Wall"—the local red earth reinforced with stones and bound with cement. It was roofed with cedar-wood tiles, called shingles,

and sheltered by a grove of trees on either side.
Besides a tall coconut palm, there were oranges,
lemons, bananas, pawpaws and ackees—Pauline
had not time to see more before Mark pulled her
through the door. It opened directly into the bedroom, which was also the living-room. The large
bed took up most of the space; there was also a
chair, a table on which stood a spirit-stove, a
wooden box, and some hanging shelves for
crockery. Everything was beautifully neat and
clean, as was the old lady propped against the
pillows, who now held out both her hands to
Pauline.

"Here she is, Granny!" cried Mark triumphantly; but the old lady was silent while she looked
at Pauline's face as if she could read her thoughts.

"I know you already, my dear," she said, at last.
"Mark has told me so much—it's as if you were
an old friend! But . . . you're not happy, child.
What's been troubling you?"

"It's because of the competition, Granny,"
Mark put in. "You know, I told you all about
her work being lost. And she nearly didn't come
to see you—'cause she was feeling so low."

"Mark tells me you think someone's played an
underhand trick on you," Mrs. Bailey said, still
holding the girl's hands and gazing searchingly
into her face. "Do you really think there's one
among your schoolfellows who'd do a mean thing
like that?"

" I know one who might have done it," muttered Pauline.

"We think she *has* done it, too! " said Mark putting Pauline's flowers into a jug of water.

" If that's so, it's going to be hard for you to act as a Christian should. Yet—we're told to forgive up to seventy times seven—which is the same as saying for ever! By the time you've forgiven a person that often, you'll have formed a habit of it; and it'll be easier to forgive than to bear malice."

" But there are some folks who *make* you quarrel with them, however much you try to keep the peace," Pauline protested. Mrs. Bailey made her sit on the one chair, while Mark perched on the box which contained all his grandmother's possessions. Then she opened the Bible which lay on the bed.

" '*Seek* peace and ensue it,' " she read. "That's more than just keeping the peace; you've got to go after it—pursue it—not just wait for it to happen of itself. The Lord made it clear that *keeping* the peace isn't enough; it's the peace*makers*, He said, which shall be called the children of God."

" But if people act mean, isn't it only fair to pay them back? " Pauline objected.

" That's the way of the world; but it's not the Christian way," replied the old lady. "Where there's peace already, there's no need for a peacemaker. But if you forgive them that injure you, and go half-way to meet them that try to quarrel with you, you'll show that you're a true child of God. It's the family likeness coming out, don't you see? 'By this shall all men know that ye are My disciples, if ye have love one to another.'"

Pauline tried to imagine herself being friendly to Jennifer—actually loving her—but somehow she couldn't see it happening.

"She's awfully poor," she said thoughtfully. " I went and had a look at her brother's house, where she lives, just to—just so as to know about her. And it looks a wretched sort of a place."

" Joe Haynes, her brother, is 'most always out of a job," added Mark. " He seems to be up against everybody, sort of."

" There are still some like that . . . even after all this long time." Mrs. Bailey spoke dreamily, as if her mind had gone back a long long way. " My father's parents were born in slavery," she explained, seeing the children look puzzled. " All the coloured folks were slaves in those days . . . taken from Africa to work on the sugar plantations; bought and sold like animals—and treated like animals, too, in some places. But not all were like that; my father's people had a good boss, and his wife taught her darkies to be Christians. She had them all into the house for prayers, night and morning, and she taught them from the Bible. She looked after them when they were sick, too, and had the children taught to read and write; so that when they became free people, they weren't so badly off as some."

"But they were all better off free, weren't they?" asked Pauline.

"You'd think so, wouldn't you, honey? But lots of them didn't know what to do with their freedom; they'd always been looked after, and told what to do and where to go. They'd spend their wages on drink; and they'd loaf around the place, stealing anything they could lay hands on. There was hatred in their hearts—hatred for the folk who had made them slaves; and they passed this hating on to their children's children . . . so that there's some to-day who go round hating everyone, without rightly knowing why."

"Joe Haynes is like that," agreed Mark. "He's got a grouch against everybody—'specially if they're well off; and he hates the English worse than anything, though I don't believe he's ever met an English person."

"I know an English lady," Pauline said shyly. "She's the wife of that Missioner who's stopping with Archdeacon; and—she's my friend."

"I've heard about those Missioners," Mrs. Bailey said eagerly, "and I've often wished I could see them. But I don't suppose they'd ever come here."

"Would you like me to tell Mistress Elliot about you?" Pauline asked. "I could go and see her now—before I go home."

" I wouldn't want her to be bothered . . . to come all this way—just for me——" the old lady began, but Pauline interrupted her.

" It won't do any harm just to *tell* her about you; she needn't come if she doesn't want to. But I'm sure she *will* want to."

Although Pauline was genuinely anxious to do a kindness to Mark's grandmother, she was also glad to have an excuse for going to see her friend. Mrs. Elliot had said : " Come whenever you like." But she felt shy, nevertheless, of turning up at the Rectory without a special reason. Even now, when she had a good excuse for coming, she hesitated when she reached the gate at the end of the Rectory drive. She was hot and dusty after the long walk from Rocky Valley; Archdeacon might be having a tea-party—or he and his visitors might be away from home, and Lilah would be short with her for coming again so soon after last time. But even as she hesitated, she heard Mrs. Elliot's voice. She seemed to be saying goodbye to someone . . . and the next moment Jennifer Haynes came down the drive towards the gate. She passed Pauline without a word—with no more than a sidelong glance from her almond-shaped eyes; and Pauline was seized with such a fit of raging jealousy as she had never known before. It was as if a hand were squeezing her heart, making it difficult for her to breathe. Mistress Elliot was *her* friend. It wasn't right that she should be wasting her time over horrid mean trash like Jennifer.

Slowly, with leaden feet, Pauline walked towards the house, turning aside into the garden when she saw Mrs. Elliot stooping over a flower-border.

"Mistress," she called softly, though her throat felt so dry, she could hardly speak. "Good evening, Mistress."

Mrs. Elliot straightened up and came to meet her.

"Pauline! I'm so glad to see you, dear. I hoped you would come."

She smiled very kindly; but Pauline dropped her eyes. She didn't want smiles or kindness, if she had got to share them with Jennifer.

"I've only come with a message," she mumbled, "It's from Mark's Granny, Mistress Bailey, the old lady what's shut in all day and can't leave her bed. I've been to see her, and she'd like you to come . . . but she's afraid to trouble you."

"It will be no trouble, and of course I'll go and see her. Archdeacon knows where she lives, I suppose? But Pauline dear—what's happened to you? You're not happy this evening, are you?"

"It's—it's that Jennifer!" Pauline burst out before she could stop herself. "I saw her coming away from here."

Mrs. Elliot smiled. "Yes, she came to the back door with a basket of fresh eggs to sell. Lilah said

she didn't need any; but the poor girl looked so
sad and disappointed, I bought them all myself!
I don't know what we shall do with them . . . but
she seemed so miserable——''

"Don't you have anything to do with her,
Mistress! She's mean and spiteful, and she lives in
a poor wretched place—with her brother, who's
real bad. She's not fit to speak to you."

Mrs. Elliot was no longer smiling, and her voice
was cold and stern as she said: "In that case, Jennifer is in special need of kindness. I'm surprised
and disappointed in you, Pauline. I thought you
wanted to follow our Lord—Who would leave
ninety and nine good people in order to go out
into the wilderness after the one who is lost."

Pauline turned away, while the burning tears
rolled down her cheeks. It was bad enough to
have to share her friend with another; but now it
seemed that she was to lose this friendship alto-
gether. And, like everything else, it was Jennifer's
fault.

"You cannot be near our Lord while you are
being hard and unforgiving to other people," Mrs.
Elliot continued. "Your angry thoughts will
separate you from Him, just as the clouds separate
you from the sun." This was what Mama had
said . . . and Mark's Granny, too. There must
be some truth in it, if all these people were agreed.
And yet—how *could* she forgive Jennifer?

"I can't! It isn't possible," she muttered.

Mrs. Elliot put her arms round her, and gently kissed her forehead.

"With God, nothing is impossible," she told her. "Ask Him to help you. He doesn't expect you to manage by yourself."

Pauline was feeling much calmer and happier when she left the garden. But at the end of the drive she paused for a minute or two, trying to remember what it was that had puzzled her, before her jealousy and Mrs. Elliot's sternness had put it out of her mind. It was something queer about Jennifer, something that Mrs. Elliot had told her, and suddenly it all came back to her; and the shock of remembering made her forget everything else that the Missioner's wife had said.

Jennifer had brought a basket of eggs; she had sold some fresh eggs to the English lady. And there were no hens—no poultry of any sort—at Jennifer's home.

Chapter 10

"IT HAS BEEN FOUND!"

WHEN she got to the school on Monday morning, Pauline found Teacher looking out for her.

"I'm glad you're early," Teacher said. "Come in here for a minute. Miss Benyon and I want to have a word with you."

As Pauline followed her into the Headmistress's tiny box-like office, she wondered nervously what she could possibly have done to deserve an interview with Miss Benyon. Had she been so very inattentive in class? Or had there been an inspection of desks? This happened quite often, and Pauline's desk was generally the untidiest in the school. Teacher was often cross with her for being so careless and unmethodical; but she had never yet sent her to Miss Benyon on that account. The Headmistress was sitting at her writing-desk, looking very grave. Teacher and Pauline stood in front of her, because there was no other chair in the room.

"I want to talk to you about your competition embroidery, Pauline," Miss Benyon said. Although she did not smile, she didn't look angry; if anything, she seemed a little embarrassed. "When you lost it, we were all very sorry for you; at the same time, we agreed that it was probably your own fault, as you are so careless with your things."

Miss Benyon paused; then went on: "However, it seems that we were wrong. Your embroidery has been found." She opened a drawer and took from it a folded white towel. As she unwrapped the towel, Pauline could not suppress a cry of joy at the sight of her precious tablecloth.

"Oh—thank you, Miss Benyon! Thank you!" she stammered. "Please—where was it? Where did you find it?"

Miss Benyon looked graver still as she replied: "It was found under a bundle of dusters in the cleaners' cupboard. It was very creased and rather dirty, but I have cleaned it as best I could, and pressed it very carefully. I don't think it is any the worse."

Pauline picked up the tablecloth and unfolded it with loving hands. Not having seen it for several days, she had forgotten how gay and pretty the silken flowers were, even in their unfinished state.

"It won't be finished for the competition," she murmured. "But oh—I *am* glad to have it safe!"

"I have two things to tell you, Pauline," the Headmistress said, "and you must listen carefully, because they're important."

"Yes, Miss Benyon."

"First, I have been forced to come to the con-
clusion that someone purposely hid your needlework, so as to prevent you from finishing it in time
for the competition."

"Ah——!" Pauline's eyes flashed, but she
kept them fixed on Miss Benyon's face, waiting to
hear what she would say. But it was Teacher who
spoke next.

"Since we believe now that it was not, after all,
your fault that the needlework was lost, you are
to be allowed to miss some of your lessons, in order
to finish this in time for the competition . . .
which, as you know, is on Tuesday week."

"*Oh*——!" Pauline's face was radiant, and
she seized Teacher's hand and kissed it; but there
was no answering happiness on the faces of her
mistresses.

"You must realize that a serious thing has happened," Miss Benyon told her. "It makes me very
sad to know that a child in my school has done this
dreadful thing. We have got to find out who has
done it."

"But—I *know*——" Pauline began, but Miss
Benyon held up her hand.

"No; I don't want you to mention any name.
There are certain children whom I shall question
privately; I have my own ways of finding out what
I want to know. But I don't wish you to have anything to do with the enquiry."

G

"Nobody came forward when I made the first announcement—that the embroidery was missing," Teacher said, "so it will be of no use to ask again in class."

"No; I think it will be better to let nobody know that it has been found—for the time being," Miss Benyon said. "I don't want a lot of gossip; that would only make it more difficult to find out what I want to know. Can you keep it to yourself, Pauline, do you think?"

Pauline nodded absently. She could not take her eyes from the delicate sprays of silky flowers, and her fingers itched to begin stitching the scarlet poinsettias.

"Do you understand, Pauline?" Teacher said, giving her a gentle shake. "You are not to tell anybody that it has been found . . . except your Mama, of course. But no one in the school is to know yet."

"You may miss all the afternoon classes, and come and work at it here, in my office," the Headmistress told her. "I don't think any of your friends will ask questions; they will think I am giving you special coaching in arithmetic—which, by the way, you badly need!" she added with a smile. "Leave your work in this drawer, now; and bring it to me here every morning when you first get to school."

When Pauline had gone, the two mistresses looked at each other in silence for a few minutes.

Then: "You are sure you know who did it?" Miss Benyon asked.

"Yes—but I've no proof," replied the other. "I don't think she'll ever confess, either; and I don't see how you are going to get the truth out of her. Why do you think it will help matters if nobody is told that the embroidery has been found?"

Miss Benyon smiled rather sadly "It was true what I told Pauline, just now—that the more gossip there is, the more difficult it may be to get at the truth," she said. "But—that was not my only reason. I don't like to have to confess that we, the staff, have so little control over these children that we might not be able to prevent the tablecloth from being stolen yet again; or, maybe, damaged beyond repair. But it's true—and you know it as well as I do!"

Teacher nodded. "We do our best . . . but there are so few of us teachers for a school this size, and the children *do* get out of hand, sometimes."

"I had another reason, too, for wanting to keep this affair secret, for the present," the Headmistress said slowly. "Rather a childish one, I'm afraid! Pauline's work is really beautifully done, considering her age, and the design is charming. I can't help wanting to have it displayed, on the day of the competition, as a surprise. A nice surprise for all her friends . . . but rather a shock for the one

who tried to play such an unkind trick on
her!"

With some difficulty, because of lack of space, a
second chair was put into Miss Benyon's office; and
on this Pauline sat and sewed every afternoon.
Sometimes Miss Benyon sat writing at her desk;
but usually she was teaching in one of the classes,
and Pauline sat alone. She had managed to keep
the secret, and nobody except her mother knew
that the needlework had been found. She couldn't
see any sense in making all this mystery, when it
seemed to her so certain that Jennifer Haynes was
the culprit. However, she didn't think about Jennifer much during these happy hours when she
stitched the lovely bright silk—long and short,
long and short—and saw the scarlet petals growing
under her hands. She couldn't help knowing that
her tablecloth was beautiful. Miss Benyon stopped
to look at it nearly every time she went in or out
of the office, and Teacher came to inspect it every
day when school was over.

She longed to tell Alice that her treasure was
safe and would certainly be finished in time to be
entered for the competition. It was still harder to
keep the news from Mark who had been so sympathetic, and from his Granny. Pauline had been
to see the old lady again, one afternoon before
going home from school. Though she grudged
every minute that was not spent at work on her

embroidery, yet the happiness and relief at having recovered it made her want to make other people happy—as a way of saying thank you.

She did try hard not to be selfish; but Mama was so anxious to see the tablecloth finished that she insisted on doing many of the home duties which were generally left to Pauline. Mrs. Cole never once complained of the extra work, and Pauline felt grateful to her, and determined to make it up to her in the future.

She was given an opportunity to do this on the day when the tablecloth was finished, and lay— neatly pressed and folded—in Miss Benyon's desk.

"I didn't like to worry you with this before, honey; but I'm awful short again this week," her mother said, when Pauline came home; "and when Doctor Barrett was in at Mistress Grant's the other day, he said that his garden's in a real bad way. Mistress Barrett would be glad of you, when-ever you can spare an hour or two."

"I'll go there now," Pauline said promptly, knowing that her mother meant that she needed money. "I can put in an hour or so, and still be home before dark. And to-morrow's Saturday; I can give her all day if she needs me."

"Maybe you'd best wait for to-morrow," Mrs. Cole said doubtfully. To reach the Barretts' house, Pauline would have to walk back to the town by the way she had just come; then through the town itself, and a quarter of a mile out on the other side. But still—" I'll go now," she decided " The walk won't hurt me; and I'll be glad of some outdoor work after all these days sitting over that embroidery."

The Barretts had the best garden for miles around, but lately Mrs. Barrett had been troubled with arthritis, while the doctor was too busy to do much work in it himself. They had often employed Pauline at odd times; they could trust her to be careful of their rare plants, and she was quick and handy with the weeding and watering.

It was a nuisance having to walk all this way when, if she had known before, she could have gone there straight from school, but gardening would make a nice change from sewing, and she looked forward to seeing what alterations had taken place since she had been there last.

She found the doctor's grey-haired wife hobbling about the garden, leaning on a stick as she gazed sadly at her precious plants.

" The poor things are dying of thirst," she complained. " Will you fetch the can, Pauline, and give them all a good soaking? Don't stint them; there's plenty of water in the catchment."

The water butt on wheels was too heavy for Pauline to manage, and it was hard work going backwards and forwards with the can, but she loved watering the plants, seeing them revive before her eyes. Mrs. Barrett was relieved to hear that she could come for the whole of the next day. "There's so much to be done,' 'she sighed. "Those orchids want separating . . . and the lilies should be staked; but you won't have time for more than the watering this evening, though I'd be glad if you'd shut the hens up before you go. I find it hard to get about these days."

In spite of the cool evening breeze, Pauline's face was soon glistening with perspiration as she toiled to and fro, carrying the heavy watering-can. Mrs. Barrett watched her for a while, then hobbled across to the lemon-tree and gathered two enormous lemons. She disappeared into the house, and soon came out with a glass of iced lemonade and a slice of cake.

"Sit down and rest for a minute," she said as she handed them to Pauline. "You've done wonders, and I'll sleep better myself to-night for knowing that my plants are comfortable. It's time you started for home, now; it'll be dark in an hour."

Pauline tipped back her head to suck down the last dregs of the delicious lemonade; then she ran off to shut the hens in, returning with three eggs she had found in the nest-boxes.

"There's a good girl!" exclaimed the doctor's wife. "I'll be glad of these; we've been very short of eggs lately."

"Our fowls are laying well," Pauline told her

proudly. "I thought everyone's did, at this time of year. You can't get any price for them in the market."

"To tell you the truth, I think someone's been after them," Mrs. Barrett said, lowering her voice. "We were getting plenty of eggs till this week; but these are the first I've seen for three days."

Pauline was very thoughtful as she left the doctor's garden, and she paused when she reached the main road. She had passed this gate when she followed Jennifer to her home. Jennifer would have to pass the Barretts' house every time she went into the town. Pauline walked slowly towards the town; then, suddenly, she broke into a trot. Mama would be furious if she were to stay out after dark; but if she hurried she might just have time to go round by Rocky Valley and be home before the light went. She needed someone to help her with what she planned to do, and Mark would be better than anybody.

She was glad to find him outside the house, digging up some sweet potatoes. Somehow she did not want to discuss her plan in front of his Granny. Silently she beckoned him away from the house and whispered to him for a long time; and as he listened to her his face broke into a delighted grin.

"I'll be there!" he chuckled. "Five o'clock, sharp"

"I'd never be allowed to come that early,"

Pauline objected. "Half-past five will be soon enough, surely?"

"I'd best be there at five," he persisted. "I'll keep watch till you come. But it'll take the two of us to do the job properly, so come along as soon as you can."

Chapter 11

CATCHING THE THIEF

TO get to the doctor's house at half-past five, Pauline had to leave her home at five o'clock, and as she had expected Mama disapproved of the idea from the start, especially as Pauline would not tell her the reason for this early expedition.

"It's something Mark Bailey and I want to do for Mistress Barrett," was all she would say. "It's a secret, Mama; I'll tell you all about it afterwards, I promise."

"I'm afraid that boy's going to lead you into mischief," Mama grumbled, "though he's not a boy who's likely to get into bad company, I'll say that for him."

All Jamaican children are warned by their parents against "getting into bad company", which is their way of describing the gangs of wild rough boys who make a habit of flouting authority and breaking the law. Mrs. Cole knew Mark's parents and guessed that Pauline would be safe with him; so she let her go, though not very willingly.

"And mind you're back in time to milk Nanny

and feed the hens," she reminded her. "It seems a crazy idea—as you'll have to go all the way back there again to work in the garden. But I can see you mean to have your own way."

The sun was just beginning to gild the distant mountain-tops when Pauline joined Mark in the hiding-place he had found at the end of the Barretts' garden. This had once been a coffee plantation, though all that remained were a few coffee-bushes and the flat paved terraces, called barbecues, on which the coffee had been spread to dry in the sun. There was a steep drop at one end of the barbecues, and, crouching here in a thicket of coffee-bushes, lemon-trees and hibiscus, the children could see without being seen. The hen-house with its wire-netting run was twenty feet away, and just beyond it was a path leading to the former slave-quarters behind the house. The Barretts' maid, Clarice, slept and cooked her own meals there, and the children could hear sounds which meant that she was preparing to go into the main building to begin her daily work.

The sun's rays had reached the garden now, but there was still a sharp, early-morning freshness in the air, and the lemon-trees smelt delicious. They heard Clarice go into the house; then there was silence, but for the songs of birds and the triumphant clucking of two hens.

"That's two eggs, for certain!" muttered Mark.

"Three, at least!" giggled Pauline, who had

heard a rustling sound from the nest-boxes. There was more clucking; the hens were certainly doing their duty this morning. But now Mark laid a warning hand over Pauline's mouth as his sharp ears detected another sound. So faint that it could hardly be heard, the pad-pad of bare feet on the gravel path told them that someone was cautiously approaching the hen-run. The two children remained perfectly still, as though frozen, while they watched Jennifer Haynes emerge stealthily from the other side of the raised barbecue. She carried a palm-leaf basket, and her eyes were fixed on the hen-house. But on reaching the entrance to the wire run, she stopped and turned to look back at the garden. The sun was shining more strongly, lighting up the delicate colours of the orchids, begonias and lilies; setting fire to the brilliant hibiscus and scarlet poinsettias, the vivid blue of the plumbago, and the golden globes on the orange-trees. On Jennifer's face was the same expression of peaceful rapture as when she had watched the humming-birds on the hillside, and Pauline caught her breath with the shock of realizing that, if circumstances had been different, she might almost have *liked* Jennifer. They both felt so much the same about certain things, that they ought to have been friends; but of course that was out of the question.

And now Jennifer had turned again towards the fowl-run. Her face was once more hard and purposeful as she undid the home-made fastening of the wire-netting door. She made a low chirruping sound which appeared to soothe and reassure the fowls, so that there was no agitated cackling and squawking as might have been expected when a stranger approached their house. Even when Jennifer raised the outside lid of the row of nest-boxes and turned a bird off one of the nests, there was no unusual commotion. As her fingers closed round a warm egg——

"*Now!*" gasped Mark, and he and Pauline made a dash for the entrance to the hen-run.

Swift and supple as a cat, Jennifer reached it before they did, and would have escaped had there not been two of them. But they closed in on her and caught her up against the wire, each seizing one of her arms. After her first shrill yelp of fear, like the cry of a hunted animal, she made no further sound, but she fought like a fury, kicking and biting and butting them with her head, trying with all her might to free her arms. She bent double to butt Mark in the stomach; straightened up and hooked her leg round Pauline's, and then all three were struggling on the ground.

"We'll—have to—tie her—arms," Mark panted. "Cord—in my pocket—I can—hold her—for a second."

Even lying on her back with wrists and ankles tied and with the other two on top of her, Jennifer did not plead for mercy. Only her terrified eyes gave her away, and her greyish pallor, while the quick rise and fall of her chest betrayed her hurried breathing.

"Can you manage alone now, while I run in and fetch Doctor Barrett?" Pauline whispered to Mark. She wanted to get away from Jennifer's eyes.

"Yes—you run in and tell them we've got her," replied the boy, sucking the back of his hand where Jennifer had bitten it. "She deserves to be locked up—the mean sneak-thief!"

"You know, you *did* hide my embroidery. And you stole my red silk, too," Pauline said, as if in answer to an appeal that had not been made aloud.

"I'll—tell you where it is . . . your embroidery . . . if you'll let me go," Jennifer muttered hoarsely, speaking for the first time since they had seen her. In the excitement of this moment of victory, Pauline completely forgot her promise to the Headmistress.

"I don't need to be told! Miss Benyon found it, days and days ago," she said triumphantly. "She let me work on it in school . . . and it's finished ! And I'm entering it for the competition on Tuesday!"

Jennifer lay quite still, as though turned to stone. Pauline had scrambled to her feet, ready to run towards the house; but first she looked down, once more, on her enemy—brought as low as she had ever wished to see her. She hadn't meant to look at Jennifer; one shouldn't look at people who are unhappy, she thought. Especially if one intends to punish them as they deserve. She shut her eyes—because she wanted to run to the house and fetch the doctor, and while she could still see Jennifer her legs would not obey her.

But when she shut her eyes, she seemed to hear the voice of her friend the English lady.

"No—don't shut your heart to the sufferings of others; don't quench your feeling of compassion. It was given you by our Lord. . . ."

"Go *on*!   What are you waiting for?" cried Mark.

He had said: "By this shall all men know that ye are My disciples, if ye have love one to another."

"Look here!   If you won't go—I shall!" Mark had come to the end of his patience, and his bitten hand was throbbing. "Sit on her—like this; and I'll go to the house."

Why did Jennifer's eyes have to look like the eyes of all the chained dogs, all the overloaded donkeys, all the ill-treated mules in the world? Why was it suddenly impossible to hate her? Impossible to feel anything but this tearing, burning pity?   Pauline dropped to her knees beside the other girl, but not to hold her down as Mark expected.

"Jennifer," she said, "if we let you go this time, will you promise—*promise*—never to steal from Mrs. Barrett again? Nor from anyone else?"

"What's the matter, girl? Are you crazy?" Mark almost shouted.

"Didn't you know that Mrs. Barrett is crippled —and nearly always in pain?" Pauline continued, her eyes on Jennifer's. "There's only Clarice, and she's busy in the house all day, and Doctor's out visiting sick folks. If people want to rob this place, there's no one to stop them."

"What's the use of giving her that kind of talk? You know she's not to be trusted," Mark said savagely.

"I think she could be trusted—if she gives us her promise now," Pauline replied. "*Will* you promise, Jennifer?"

"I—promise." It was no more than a whisper. "Let me go—this once—and I'll never do it again."

Mark grasped Pauline's hands which were picking at the knot that bound Jennifer's wrists.

"I don't know what's come over you!" he exclaimed. "You *can't* want to let her off—when she's acted so mean to you, taking your tablecloth, trying to spoil your chances for the competition. She deserves to be punished for that far more than for pinching a few eggs."

"I don't want her punished." Pauline spoke in a low voice, and her tears fell on Jennifer's hands.

"It's no good, Mark, I can't explain. It's just—
I can't bear to see her like this."

"I suppose you know you're letting *us* in for a
lot of trouble, if you're soft enough to let her go,"
he told her sternly. "Helping a thief to get
away . . . that's being a—a—a party to the crime,
that's what it's called. And I can't think *why*
you're being so daft."

"I can't tell you why—because I don't know
myself. I only know—that I can't bear to have
her like this. I *want* her to be let off."

"*Well!*" Mark scrambled to his feet and
shrugged his shoulders. He had always heard that
girls were extraordinary creatures; that it was impossible to understand them, and no use trying to
work with them. And now he knew it was true.

"Help me undo these knots, Mark," she pleaded.
"Clarice will be out to feed the hens soon. Do
help me, please."

Jennifer did not attempt to thank them, nor to
say she was sorry, when they released her and
helped her to her feet. She gave one look at
Pauline—a look which said a great deal; then she
was gone, running noiselessly down the narrow
path which led to the back gate.

Jennifer Haynes was the last person Miss Benyon
expected to find waiting outside her office on Monday morning. She had expected this particular
girl to avoid her, and all the other members of the

H

staff; but here was Jennifer asking to speak to her privately.

"Please, Miss Benyon," she said, when they were inside the office and the door shut. "I've come to tell you—I don't want to enter my place-mats for the competition to-morrow."

"You wish to withdraw your entry?" the Headmistress asked gravely. "Why is that, Jennifer? You had a good chance of winning the first prize, you know."

"I don't want to enter it," the girl repeated stubbornly.

"But—*why*?" Like everyone else concerned, Miss Benyon suspected Jennifer of having hidden Pauline's entry. This sudden decision might be due to an attack of conscience; but what she already knew of Jennifer did not make it seem likely. If it were true, however, and if she had behaved in such a dishonest way to one of her rivals, it was only fair that she should withdraw her entry from the competition.

But Jennifer, when questioned, merely repeated: "I'd rather not say," again and again, and finally refused to answer at all.

Miss Benyon was in a quandary. She was proud of the high standard of handwork done in her school. The Inspector of Schools and the wife of the Custos were coming to judge the competition, and she had looked forward to displaying the embroidery section, which was particularly good this year. The withdrawal of Jennifer's place-mats would be a sad blow to her pride . . . but she knew she ought not to consider that; and in any case, since the girl obstinately refused to exhibit them, there was no more to be said.

If anyone had been able to prove that Jennifer had been the culprit where Pauline's work was concerned, the place-mats would have been disqualified as a matter of course. And now she had disqualified them herself—though refusing to give any reason for this surprising decision.

Chapter 12

THE COMPETITION

THE day of the competition was always a whole holiday for the school. The children whose parents had gardens brought flowers, and helped in the decoration of the classrooms, and a few of the bigger girls helped the teachers to arrange the exhibits on trestle-tables. These consisted of carpentry, woodcarving, painting, hand-weaving and basket-work, as well as dressmaking and embroidery, and the younger children had a long trestle-table to themselves on which their raffia-work and elementary painting and needlework were displayed.

There was a good deal of whispering among the girls when it was discovered that Jennifer's place-mats were not among the embroidery exhibits. Jennifer herself was nowhere to be seen, and nobody seemed to know where she was. But even without her entry, the embroidery section made an imposing array. There were table-runners, children's dresses, aprons embroidered with donkeys, flowers and orange-trees; hand-towels, mats and work-bags. In the centre was Alice's linen bedspread in drawnthread work, less colourful than Pauline's table-cloth, but so beautifully worked that there was always a small crowd in front of it, gazing at it in admiration. From midday onwards, the children's parents drifted into the school, to wander about the classrooms and exclaim over the exhibits. The guests of honour arrived at two o'clock. Chief of these was the Custos and his wife, and the Inspector, who were also the judges. Archdeacon was always present on these occasions; and this time he brought with him his two visitors, Mr. and Mrs. Elliot.

Pauline kept her eyes on Mrs. Elliot, and longed to go and speak to her, but there was no opportunity for this. The guests climbed on to the teacher's rostrum at the end of the largest class-room, and then the speeches began. Archdeacon said a prayer, and all the children sang a hymn: "Now thank we all our God." Then the Custos made a short speech, and the Schools Inspector made a long one. The Headmistress said a few words, after which she asked the children and the parents to go out into the playground and wait there until the judging had taken place.

Once the children were outside, there was a rush to buy "icicles" at the bakery, as it was very hot in the treeless playground. Their mothers sat on the steps and fanned themselves. While they praised the exhibits of other people's children, each

privately believed that her own "pickney" deserved the first prize.

People kept coming up to Pauline's mother and
saying: "Your girl should be first in the embroidery section, Mistress Cole. That's a lovely
piece of work she's done! She'll get the prize,
that's certain." And Mrs. Cole would laugh and
shake her head, and quickly say something in praise
of the other entries

It seemed a long time to wait, but at last the
school bell summoned them into the long classroom where the judges had already mounted the
rostrum.

The wife of the Custos made the first announcement. After a few words of congratulation on the
high standard of the needlework, she said: " I have
great pleasure in awarding the first prize for the
needlework section to Alice Wilson. Her bedspread of drawnthread linen is a beautiful piece of
work, and a credit to the school."

There was a storm of clapping as Alice walked
up to the rostrum to receive the certificate and the
money prize Her gentle, unselfish nature made
her popular with the whole school, though many
of the children were surprised that her exhibit
should have been preferred to Pauline's gay tablecloth.

Pauline herself joined in the clapping, though
for a moment she had thought that she was going to
faint.

She had not been conscious of any great certainty that she would win; and it was only now that she realized how much she had counted on getting the first prize. She was so stunned with the shock that she did not hear the results of the other competitions announced by the Inspector . . . the woodwork and painting, and the junior section. This, then, was the end of all the weeks of hard work and anxiety, of the drama surrounding her entry to the needlework competition. It had all been for nothing. She had not won the prize after all. She had bent her head; but her mother nudged her to make her look up, as the wife of the Custos was speaking again.

"I am going to do something rather unusual," she said. "With the permission of your Headmistress, I am personally giving an extra prize to an entry in the Needlework Section. I had great difficulty in making up my mind between two of the exhibits, because both were so excellent. But I finally awarded the first prize of one pound to Alice Wilson, because she had put so much fine work into her bedspread, and had done this work so beautifully. However, Pauline Cole's exhibit deserves a special mention, and I was so charmed by the choice of colours and the arrangement of the design in her tablecloth that I have great pleasure in awarding her this extra prize of ten shillings "

Smiling, she held up an envelope containing the

money, and another storm of applause showed how much her gesture was approved of by the school.

Pauline felt as if her legs would hardly carry her as far as the rostrum, but she was very happy when she returned to her seat beside Mama, clutching the envelope. Her tablecloth had been noticed and given a special mention, and though she had not secured the first prize, yet ten shillings would be very useful, and Mama would be glad of it.

When the prize-giving ceremony was over, Miss Benyon beckoned to Pauline.

"Mrs. Elliot wants to speak to you," she told her. "She has asked me if your tablecloth is for sale, as she wants to buy it and take it back to England. She will give you thirty shillings for it, if your Mama agrees" She went over to Mrs. Cole, while Mrs. Elliot came up to Pauline

"I think your cloth is really lovely," she said. "I wanted to buy it to give to a friend in England, as a wedding present. But I have taken such a fancy to it I really feel I must keep it myself, and find something else for my friend!"

At first, Pauline was unable to say anything, and could only nod her head in agreement while her mother and Miss Benyon settled the matter with Mrs. Elliot. She could scarcely believe her ears. Thirty shillings! With the ten shilling prize as well, she would have two pounds! There would be new shoes for Julie as well as for herself, and plenty left to put by for those times when Mama was "short".

Her tablecloth was to go all the way to England. It was to be used by Mistress Elliot, her friend, who had told Mama she was so glad to have something to remind her of Pauline.

She was sent to fetch the cloth and wrap it up; and by the time she had found a clean piece of paper and done it up in a neat parcel, her mother and Miss Benyon had both gone off to talk to other people, and Mrs. Elliot was alone.

"Please, Mistress, there's something I want to ask you," Pauline said shyly, as she handed the parcel to the Missioner's wife. "You—you said you'd be looking out for something to give for a wedding present. Would you think of buying a lovely set of place-mats, what was never put in the competition? They're ever so pretty: I think they might have got first prize, if they'd been put in."

"I'd certainly like to see them," Mrs. Elliot replied. "Is this some more of your own work?"

"No, Mistress. They were done by a—a friend of mine. They were meant for the competition . . . but—she changed her mind—at the last minute."

"And are they as beautifully worked as your cloth?"

"I believe they're better, really," Pauline said truthfully. "And she needs the money real bad."

"Where is this friend of yours? Would she

bring the mats to show me?" Mrs. Elliot asked, looking round at the ever-moving crowd of children in their brightly-coloured cotton dresses.

"She's not here, to-day." Pauline hesitated, then added: "It's Jennifer Haynes—the girl who came to the Rectory that day——"

"Jennifer Haynes! Yes, I remember her, of course." Mrs. Elliot looked surprised. "But—I thought . . ."

"Yes," Pauline admitted, hanging her head. "We had a quarrel; but—we've made peace, now. I think, I'm not sure, but I think we're going to be friends."

Chapter 13

JAMAICAN FAREWELL

IT was the last open-air service of the Mission. For the last time, the crowd round the village store had heard Archdeacon's gramophone as the car sped up the road. It was playing the hymn: "Hark, hark my soul," which had become a favourite during the Mission: and when the car pulled up, everyone was singing the words:

"Onward we go, for still we hear them singing—
Come, weary souls, for Jesus bids you come.
. . . The music of the Gospel brings us home."

After Archdeacon had said the prayers, the Missioner preached his last sermon, while his wife let her eyes wander over the row of dark faces which had become so dear to her. No longer were they the faces of strangers. Many of these people had come to the services night after night; some had talked with her after the service was over, or had come to see her at the Rectory,

To-night, during the reading of the words: "By this shall all men know that ye are my disciples, if

ye have love one to another," Mrs. Elliot saw a girl
in a red-and-white striped dress grasp the hand of
of the taller girl standing next to her.

She had learnt a great deal about Pauline during
the two days since the competition.   Old Mrs.
Bailey had heard, from Mark, the whole story of
the theft of Pauline's embroidery, and of how
Pauline had forgiven Jennifer and refused to have
her punished.   Mark's Granny had repeated all
this to Mrs. Elliot, who knew that Jennifer was
now on a visit to the Coles, sharing Pauline's bed
and going with her to school each day.   It was to
Pauline's home that Mrs. Elliot had gone to buy
Jennifer's place-mats; and she knew that the two
girls had intended to come to the last Mission service together.

It was sad to know that this was her last night in
dear Jamaica.   Short as her stay had been, in no
other place in the world had she felt so much at
home.   A part of her would always belong to this
beautiful island and to its warm-hearted people.

There was a hush before the singing of the last
hymn . . . after the Missioner had asked if there
were any here who had not yet "come home".
Silence—but for the chirping of the crickets and
"singing-frogs", that chorus which is so much part
of the Jamaican night that you cease to notice it.
Then, very softly, the crowd began to sing: "Rock
of Ages".   Their bodies swayed while they sang,
and some of them sung the hymn kneeling.   At

the words "Nothing in my hand I bring; simply to Thy Cross I cling"—Jennifer dropped to her knees and Pauline knelt beside her, with their hands still tightly clasped.

The goodbyes were said; the last handshakes exchanged; Archdeacon's car with the Missioners started down the hill on its homeward journey. A record of "Love Divine", sung to the joyous Welsh tune, was broadcasting from the loudspeaker. Softly, more softly, very faint now—but still it could be heard; and the singing was taken up by those going up the hill and down the hill to their homes, so that the night was full of music.

Pauline and Jennifer, straining to hear the last sounds from the car, gave it up and joined in the singing.

"And it was nicer like that," Pauline said to Jennifer afterwards. "We never exactly knew when they'd quite, quite gone; so it's as if they'd never really left us at all."